CW00420508

HIDDEN
SECRETS

IvanB

DEDICATION

To Ann

Author contact
ivanb@btinternet.com

Cover Illustration
Data Cedes ©2023 IvanB

CONTENTS

Last Meet

We met at the viewing point, a paved area on the cliff top where there are six benches, a couple of explanatory geographical mosaics, two memorial plaques, and the inevitable £2 in the slot telescope. It is all a bit of a misnomer as there is only the sea to see, the cliff is only fifteen metres high, and it is on the edge of the residential area as tourists are confined to the promenade below. There was a large container ship going south towards Felixstowe and a two-masted yacht tacking into the wind, otherwise, the sea was bare, apart from a flock of seagulls wheeling and squawking on their way to intimidating the unwary. He came and sat down next to me and silently handed me a brown paper bag containing a fancy chicken roll, with salad and basil mayonnaise, plus a USB memory stick hidden in the second paper napkin. As usual, he was in an old Barbour brown wax jacket with an accompanying brown flat cap, but his hangdog face looked even more hangdog, and the sigh as he sat was deeper than usual. We tucked in; me with the roll and him cutting slices off a pork pie with his well-worn penknife.

"Family all right?" he grunted.

"Running around nicely," I replied.

He nodded and glanced around, but no one else was joining us in late May with a stiff easterly breeze. He stretched his legs out.

"Last meal," he announced. "I'm moving on."

This was a surprise.

"You never said," I chided.

"Political," he half-spat.

I knew that I could not ask.

"Shame, I'll have to eat by myself."

He grimaced.

"My daughter said she would keep an eye on you, she likes to be called Yvette. You might want to meet her at The Piazza Espresso Bar, she looks like a waitress, but has a string of black pearls and a floral painting on her left hand; she's just back from Casablanca." He gave a false laugh. "She was trekking and is still a mite wet behind the ears."

I nodded.

"Will our paths cross again?" I murmured.

"Only if there is a revolution and the bourgeoisie are lined up against the wall and shot."

I managed a laugh.

"Then I could still send you a dead letter."

He sighed.

"This is a prime spot; I shall miss it."

He scrunched up his brown bag.

"Fancy your dessert?" I asked.

He sniffed.

"Might as well take it away."

I handed him a large pear, that he tucked in a pocket

before he stood up.

"Be good," he said. "And try not to be a doormat."

He wandered off and I bit into my pear. He'd been my handler for five years, and I don't like change.

Liaison

The Piazza is a large, paved area across the sea end of our two parallel high streets, North and South Boulevard. During the summer it is a happy place with cafes overflowing onto the pavements, an ice-cream vendor at the top of Windy Road that goes down to the beach, and people sitting on the sea-facing benches having picnics or enjoying the sunshine. Winter turns it bleak, and even now in early Spring only The Piazza Espresso Bar had tables out on the pavement, but they have a glass awning and patio heaters. It is a long café taking up four shop fronts, but she was easy to spot as she had a knee-length black dress, black ankle boots and a single string of black pearls. I hung back a bit to get a fuller picture. Straight shoulder length mousy coloured hair, black cotton gloves and a soft black handbag big enough to hide a 9mm pistol. I wandered across and smiled.

"Of all the gin joints in all the towns in all the world, she walks into mine," I paused. "Good Holiday?"

She studied me with her amber, almost yellow, eyes.

"I remember every detail. The Germans wore gray," She flashed a wide-mouthed smile. "But I didn't like the venue because, without freedom of choice, there is no creativity."

Her accent was pure Devon and I wondered what she felt about my Welsh Valley's intonation.

"Perhaps, the needs of the many outweigh the needs of the few," I responded.

She relaxed as we'd done the Casablanca and Star Trek interchanges, but I was still not satisfied and switched to a fall-back, dear old Maggie Thatcher.

"It is said that; there is no such thing as society: there are individual men and women, and there are families."

Her eyes narrowed.

"I don't mind how much my Ministers talk, so long as they do what I say."

I nodded.

"Any additions while you have been away?" I asked casually.

She frowned and then peeled back her left glove so I could see a stylised piece of body painting of a rose, complete with a few thorns.

"Looks painful," I muttered.

She huffed.

"Not as painful as a double knee and ankle replacement, but since you are wearing shorts, I do not have to ask you to reveal yourself."

A waitress appeared and we ordered coffee and flapjack; I waited.

She glanced around to make sure there was no one on adjacent tables.

"Just let me check, you are still not in a permanent

relationship?"

"I didn't know this would be a vetting check," I replied brusquely.

Her arching eyebrows rose.

"I dictate what we do and what we don't do. Your former manager said that you hung about with a woman called Yesterday, but she is a security risk because of her background. I trust that has not matured into a relationship, because if it does, I might have to lower your security rating."

I glared at her.

"You do not employ me, and you are not, and never will be, my boss and what I do or do not do in my spare time is of no concern to you," I growled.

"If you want to stay in work, then it does concern us; and you'd better believe it" she snapped.

I stayed silent; she grimaced.

"This will be our only meet this year as I prefer dead letters, it is safer." She purred.

"I don't," I replied.

"It is not up to you." She cuttingly replied.

"Really," I said. "It takes two to tango, and at the moment we are not even hearing the same tune."

I stood up and walked away, leaving her to pay the bill.

Changed Church

I arrived at the large, cavernous red brick church that I think of as my own, to find many more people than usual milling about and standing in small groups. I squeezed behind one such group and entered our sound cage. It is not really a cage, but when they built the church at the end of the nineteenth century the designers, for some reason no one knows, placed the super-sized font in a caged area in the southwest corner of the church against the rear wall. They made the cage by using two large wrought iron fences to close off the corner. The font has since been moved, but it makes a perfect area for our sound system as it can be locked, and the church is always open from dawn to dusk. Yesterday, who preferred to be called Yaz, was already booting up the system, or rather as the system is 1970s electronics, warming up is more apt. As always, she was in light grey jeans, a lighter grey long-sleeved tee-shirt, large red dangly earrings, snow-white rather tatty trainers, and her dark hair in a long ponytail. She looked up as I wandered in.

"Who are all these people," I croaked. "Is it a special service?"

She rolled her deep brown eyes.

"Oh Allan, you are hopeless; we now have the congregation of St James joining us as their church has started to fall apart. We are now St Jude's with St James';

it's all been in the church magazine, and we did have two special church meetings about it," I detected that her slight Eastern European accent might contain an element of chiding.

"I thought it was years away."

She sighed.

"So did they, but a corner of the church was undermined in last year's heavy rains and now the ground is drying out, large cracks are appearing, so everything was brought forward, Vera did announce it last week."

I nodded as she pointed.

"We have lost channel nine."

I checked the light display and sector nine on the sound desk was not showing any lights at all. I turned off the sound desk.

"Done that, twice," she murmured. "It needs your touch."

I took a small screwdriver out of a little drawer and released the clip to let me pull out the relevant circuit board. Nothing looked burnt, so I cleaned the contacts on the edge of the board, pushed it back firmly and turned the desk on. We were rewarded with a complete set of lights.

"Rev Vera on mike A, and Rev Larry on mike C," she murmured.

"Rev Larry?" I queried.

"St James' curate, he's had to manage the transition, and this is his last Sunday," she murmured.

The organ suddenly started playing and I began to relax, Yaz was quite capable of operating the sound desk and phasing the appropriate microphones in and out, I just had to guard the overall sound level as the system was quite capable of going into full feedback with no warning at all and had a predilection to pick up broadcasts from our local taxi service.

"Talked to Stephanie, she looked after the sound at St James', she doesn't want to get involved here, but she did bring over three radio lapel mikes, two static mikes and her induction loop driver," Yaz murmured.

I sat up.

"We could do with that for the Lady Chapel."

She giggled.

"The lapel mikes would work better there if we…"

She stopped because the vestry door opened, and the show was about to hit the road; or should I say, the formal worship was about to begin.

Yaz brought back two cups of coffee and two pieces of shortbread and carefully put them on a small table away from the desk. She knew that I preferred to have my after-service coffee here and not venture into the mêlée in the North Aisle. She fingered the lapel mikes, which were far superior to our somewhat cheap 'West End musical' face mikes.

"We need to add these into our system," she said to herself.

"Do it this afternoon, if you're free," I remarked.

"If you want," she replied.

I tried to look her in the eyes.

"It depends if you were doing something important."

She shook her head.

"They have taken the ice hockey matches off ITV2 as there is extra football and I cannot get the AllSports Internet channel, in any case, the other girls like to watch their Sunday afternoon Weepies."

"Two o'clock?" I asked.

She nodded and sat down on the stool next to me.

I listened to the growl of thunder and pondered what Yvette had said. Yesterday had wandered into the church about eighteen months ago and a few months later volunteered to operate the sound desk with me when Pat moved away. I knew that she shared a three-bedroom trailer with two other women, and worked at a greengrocer, but little else and had no idea why Yvette was so anti. Her nose was somewhat prominent, her mouth a little small, her thick black eyebrows almost met in the middle, her skin tone was matt beige, and she did not understand idioms, but I was beginning to find her rather attractive. I decided to break the habits of a lifetime.

"I can't let you cycle home in this weather, how do you fancy coming to mine, I'll get lunch then you can watch ice hockey on my TV."

Her left eyebrow twitched.

"You are inviting me to your home?" She said with a mystical edge to her voice.

She gave a slight giggle.

"Rhona said that you never invite anyone into your house, she went out with you for three months, but you never invited her to yours once."

I recalled that my lack of trust may have led to our downfall. I gave a small shrug.

"The offer is still open."

She gave a small bow.

"Then I accept, but remember I am watching my waistline."

I glanced at the wide black belt around her waist that had a non-adjustable circular clasp.

"It is worth watching," I said drolly.

She frowned.

"You think I am fat?"

I shook my head.

"Not at all, I meant…"

She raised a hand.

"English is for the English; I have been taking lessons

from my housemates on puns, wordplay, and malapropisms, but it is all confusing. They say I must imagine that I am an alien from the planet Zog and I must adapt, but there is no planet Zog."

I laughed.

"There is no planet Zog, it just means somewhere far away and in a different reality."

She rolled her eyes.

"Let's stick your bicycle in the lobby and have dinner," I suggested, with the best smile I could manage

She picked up her faded blue mini-tote bag and we left, after carefully locking our 'cage.'

Home Sweet Home

I parked on the driveway, and she surveyed the end of my bungalow with its slightly offset front door and large picture window. Her foot movement during the journey told me that she probably did not drive as most drivers found sitting on the outside of my left-hand drive pickup quite disturbing.

"Why do you have a pickup?" She suddenly asked. "You are not a builder or a lumberjack, do you just like to be…"

She frowned as she could not think of the English word.

"I had a bad accident," I said truthfully. "I can't afford to be in a car accident and damage my legs again, and this is a nice safe vehicle."

She nodded.

"Rhona said you were in hospital for weeks and stayed in a rehabilitation centre until this bungalow was finished."

I wondered what else Rhona had said.

"Not so much finished as rebuilt, it was burnt down and rather a mess when I bought it."

She nodded and seemed satisfied with that and climbed out.

I let her into the hallway that has stairs going up and a short corridor that led to the bathroom door.

"Small bedroom on the left and lounge on the right," I

murmured as I opened the lounge door, and she sighed as she stepped in.

"It is big and airy."

I stepped beside her.

"Runs all the way through, so it is a lounge cum dining room cum kitchen. It made it easy for me to get about when I used a walking frame."

I walked through the lounge, which only had a three-piece suite, down through the dining room, which did not have a table, across the kitchen, which did have a pull-out breakfast bar, and out the back door. She followed me and then gasped. I'm not surprised as I have a conservatory on the back and the view is of a slightly sloping garden, and then the links golf course and the sea beyond.

"That is a view to die for," she murmured.

I smiled, but I had almost died and bought the house and pickup truck out of my compensation, along with a computer or two.

"Have an explore," I said. "I'll just put the cookpot on." She moved back into the lounge, and I opened the fridge to take out two pouches of goulash. I hesitated as in my opinion, the portions were small, and I did not want to appear to be mean. I added a third pouch and busied myself in dropping the contents of the pouches into my cookpot, adding some dried mushrooms, half a pint of milk, a dash of Worcestershire sauce, and a few almond flakes, before screwing down the lid to finally set the timer. I then popped some frozen pitta bread in the oven and paused. She had gone out of the lounge, but not reappeared or gone upstairs, and I would have known if she had gone upstairs because the stairs creaked by design.

I found her in the hall with the under-stairs door open and staring at my security door. She looked at me, and I realised that she had gone pale.

"You have a special locked door in your own house," she babbled. "Why would anyone have a locked door in their own house?" Her eyes widened. "Are you a secret pervert who hoards pornography, maybe even shoots pornography!" She exclaimed as she started to panic.

I tried to keep my voice level.

"I work from home and some of it is commercially secure."

That was an understatement, but I hoped…

"But what do you do!" she jabbered. "Rhona did not know what you do because you never told her, just said, 'something with computers.' Do you run a porno channel or…"

I moved forward and she shrank away against the bathroom door. I place my thumb on the fingerprint reader and pressed a six-digit code. There was a satisfying clunk, and I pushed the door open until it locked open against the wall.

"Take a look, I have nothing to hide," I said as reassuringly as I could.

I stepped back and she visibly trembled; clearly, she was not going anywhere.

"How about I go down first?" I murmured. "I will walk to the far end and promise not to get between you and the exit."

I did not tell her that there was a hidden second exit, as I thought that would make matters worse. I went down first, passed my computer gear, and automatically noted that my old Blackberry Playbook was indicating that search 1 was 89% complete, with three results and due to finish in two days. Search 2 was 50% complete with no results, and due to finish in three days, and search 3 was 78% complete, had yielded six results, and was due to complete in six hours. I stood at the far end, and she tentatively came down the stairs. It occurred to me that if Yvette knew of this breach in protocol, she would probably throw a hissy fit and possibly toss me to the wolves, but I did not want Yaz to think I was doing anything seedy.

Eventually, she stood in the middle of the basement. "There are a lot of computers," she mumbled.

I nodded.

"Three Mac Pro computers working as a triad. Three

Mac Studio computers doing the same. Likewise, the three Mac-minis. I control them from the 24" iMac and use the MacBooks to do other work.

"You are a hacker; you infect other people's computers with viruses" she gasped.

I shook my head.

"I am a data miner. I trawl through databases looking for certain information. It is not over-sophisticated, and time is usually on my side."

I tapped the stack of Mac minis.

"These are seeking out people who are shirking their responsibility and have avoided paying child maintenance for a long time."

She glanced upwards.

"You have radiators on the ceiling?"

"Heat extraction, I use it to supplement warming my hot tank."

She blinked and I hoped that she didn't realise that I would produce most heat in the summer, which was just when my central heating system would not use it. She closed her eyes.

"Please, I would like to go upstairs; I do not like it here. You are big brother watching people."

I took a deep breath.

"No watching involved; I am seeking out miscreants."

She stared at me.

"The Nazis called Jews miscreants; the Russians called

the Romani people…"

I jumped in before she got to our government.

"I am not supplementing persecution, I am usually finding people who left their families and are denying their responsibilities," I said evenly.

She sighed and nodded, but still made for the staircase.

When I got to the top, she was checking out the bedrooms, but I knew that all she'd find were my rather spartan bedroom and a spare bedroom with just a single bed and dressing table. She came down the creaky stairs.

"There is a cupboard on your landing," she said. "I could not open the door."

"It's tri-fold," I replied. "It is the airing cupboard and hot water tank; the cold tank is in the small roof space.

She went into the downstairs bedroom, and I heard a gasp. I went to the doorway to see her staring at the huge TV screen at the other end of the room.

"I bought it in a sale of items from a pub that was closing down; I rather like watching movies and with a screen like that, I can lose myself in the story." I paused. "I'll put your ice hockey on here, I've checked the time, we have forty minutes before kick-off."

"Face-off," she replied. "Kicking is not allowed."

Dinner

We sat at the bamboo table in my conservatory, using two of the three bamboo chairs. Before we tucked in, she insisted on saying grace and I hoped it was not a reflection on my culinary skills. Suddenly she stopped eating.

"I am sorry, I over-reacted, but I do not like basements. I know you are a kind man because I have seen you helping Mrs Chisolm with her walker and getting her coffee, even though you are not good in crowds."

I swallowed.

"I am still not very stable at times, and crowds worry me."

She recommenced eating.

"But I'd rather you don't tell anyone about my basement, the people who pay me like anonymity," I said softly.

She nodded but did not reply.

"Why do you not like basements?" I asked because I hadn't got a clue what to talk about.

She ate a few more mouthfuls before she spoke.

"My father was a Romani, and my mother was Northern Irish, but she left when I was six. One day we moved on and she stayed behind, she did not tell me why, but looking back I can guess. My father shacked up with another woman called Chantelle, she was Romani, and she resented my presence because she wanted her child to have precedence and the better bunk, even though she was a girl. Had she been a boy there would have been no question, but as a girl, she had no claim on my position." Yaz frowned. "That is unfair because it makes my father sound hard, but I know he loved me, just like he had loved mother, even though she was not a full-blood Roma."

She finished her bread.

"One day I annoyed Chantelle by telling her that she would never be my mother because my mother had blonde hair and hers always looked greasy. We were parked up by some old buildings and she responded by locking me in a basement and leaving me there. They all broke camp at noon and moved on and she left me behind. I thought I was going to die in that basement along with the dead rats and the manky mice. She claimed she forgot I was there, and father came back for me that night, but by then…" She stopped. "So, I do not like basements because they bring back memories I would rather not have." She closed her eyes. "There is more, but not now."

She opened her eyes again after a few seconds.

"Rhona never told me what your bad accident was."

I was stuffed and mounted, she had just told me of her childhood trauma, and I needed to reciprocate.

"In the graveyard entrance from the track beside the

vicarage is a drain and a hearse parked on the cover and it gave way through age. I went to a builder's yard to get a new cover and they were at the end of the yard. Halfway down a stack of timber, I saw a cat and I stopped to stroke it. Also in the yard was a forklift carrying two bags of cement, the driver lost control and the forklift did a pirouette to perfectly smash its tines into the back of my legs at knee height and grind them into the timber. I am told the driver fell off, but he climbed back on and threw it into reverse, promptly dropping the top bag of cement onto my left ankle. I lost an awful lot of blood and ended up having a double knee replacement and a new ankle joint. I was in hospital for four weeks because of a reaction to the antibiotics, and then in a rehabilitation centre for six weeks." I paused, trying not to remember the beginning of my time there. "The lad driving the forklift was seventeen, did not have a driving licence, and had only had twenty minutes of instruction. The Health and Safety Executive threw the book at the owners and gave them a whopping fine. After that, they did not fancy a prolonged case about compensation and made me an offer I couldn't refuse. It paid for this house, my truck, and a lot of the gear below. Personally, I'd rather have my old knees back and be able to walk without the fear of falling over."

She blinked.

"That makes my basement experience seem trivial."

I reached out and held her hand.

"It was not trivial to you as you still bear the scars, but I promise I will never lock you in my basement or ask you to go down there."

I thought she might pull her hand away, but she didn't, and I was surprised and how much comfort her touch gave me.

I finished stacking the dishwasher and made two mugs of tea that I took into my TV room. The room has the TV, its sound system, and some attendant boxes, plus a two-seat settee as far away from the TV as possible and my personal computer on a small desk in the corner. I sat down next to Yaz and handed her a tea. She sniffed it.

"Half a teaspoonful of brown sugar," I murmured.

"You are spoiling me," she said without her eyes leaving the screen.

"How's it going?"

"Third period; Bulgaria 3, Estonia 2," she murmured.

I watched the screen. She had said that kicking was not allowed but smashing your opponent into the ringside wall or squashing her in a pincer movement seemed fair game. Suddenly the ref made a signal, and a klaxon blew causing both sides to skate off the rink.

"I thought blood sports were banned," I said dryly.

She frowned.

"That is a joke?"

I nodded and she sighed.

"Where is it being played?" I asked, feigning interest.

"The Winter Sports Palace in Sofia," she replied. "I have been there with my father. He loves ice hockey and I think he would have liked to play. When we could we always went to matches, it was the only thing we ever did together."

We watched a few adverts, listened to some inane Canadian commentators, and some more adverts, and the game recommenced. I understand football but am not keen on it, I like the short form of cricket, I avidly watch Formula One and I try to avoid tennis as I find matches to drawn out. However, I know nothing about ice hockey and the rules, beyond the scoring, are a mystery. We sat side by side and it was apparent that she was mentally supporting Bulgaria because she let out a rising series of 'ohs' as they attacked, and muttered 'no, no, no' when Estonia progressed towards the Bulgarian goal. Halfway through There was a mêlée around the Bulgarian goal and she grabbed my hand to almost squeeze it to death, someone swiped the puck and somehow the Bulgarian goalie deflected the shot with his stick, and she sighed with relief. Three minutes later the Estonia goalie was not so lucky as there was a writhing huddle around the goalmouth and suddenly the puck was in the back of the net. She let go of my hand and clapped hers together before relaxing slightly and holding my hand again. It was this second, natural, taking of my hand that made me feel good. The game finished and she sighed.

"I could almost be there," she murmured. "Smelling the ice and being jostled in the crowd."

"Was that the final?" I asked casually but having done my research.

"No, that is Wednesday at 7:30," she replied.

"Well I guess that is a date then, I'll break out the popcorn."

She smiled, with a twinkle in her eye.

"One does not have popcorn, you have a greasy burger with fried onions, or a strong meat pie, or stew in little paper dishes, perhaps even a hot dog." She frowned. "You said a date, was that just an expression of an appointment?"

"It is time with you," I said, rather pathetically.

She nodded.

"Then on Wednesday I shall spend time with you, burgers are not necessary."

Monday - Second Meet

Monday morning, I settled down at my basement desk, search 3 had now finished and had yielded two results, which meant it had written off four results as being improbable. I checked the results, did a little bit of surfing, and consulted my notes before I made a phone call.

"DI Jacobs?" I queried as the person answered.

I nodded to myself.

"It's Allan from Hidden Secrets, you sent me a request number SP0017/B to look for an Earnest Smith and gave me a few details. Based on what you gave me, I think I have found him. He has the same academic profile, now calls himself Bert Smyth and works for an architect practice. He has a picture on the website, the eyes are a bit bluer, but he could have used Photoshop, but the central furrow in his forehead is present and correct. Do you wish to accept my findings?"

I smiled at the answer because the police paid for information, not correct results.

"I'll email them to you now."

I sent off the email and studied the USB stick I had acquired from Pete, my previous handler. It was a multi-faceted problem covering a wide scope of databases. I set about writing a small programme to attach to my general database mining routines knowing that I'd have to wait until Search 1, on my most powerful machines, completed the following day as it was too big a problem for my other triads. At precisely 11:30 an encrypted email from The Kollectors Corporation dropped in my inbox.

'We have noticed that you have placed a collector's plate in your basket, but have not completed the purchase. This can be accessed until noon today, when due to high demand, we shall remove your ability to purchase. The plate you have chosen has a unique labyrinth design with a Greek high-quality glaze and our unique logo. Do not miss out or you can only be disappointed.'

I sat back and closed my eyes. Yvette wanted a second bout.

This time she was sitting under the awning at the back of The Warren public house supposedly reading a book. I sat down.

"Books give a soul to the universe, wings to the mind, flight to the imagination, and life to everything,"' I said with a smile.

She put the book down.

"They are 'A library of wisdom, more precious than all wealth.'" She responded.

It was a slight misquote, but I let it slide.

"You don't need a book because 'the strongest logos tell simple stories," I added.

"Ah." She sighed. "But 'a logo is the period at the end

of a sentence, not the sentence itself.'"

I decided to miss out the quotes from China. She took a sip from her apple juice while I let my cider stand for a bit.

"You should learn your place," she said with an edge to her voice. "You are but a small cog in a large machine and it can run without you."

I sipped my cider.

"Perhaps the slightly bigger cogs should be wary that they don't get worn down and become lesser cogs," I murmured.

She glared at me.

"It is quite simple. We use dead letter communication, you keep your nose clean, and we can have a happy relationship, otherwise I shall file for divorce."

I drank a little more.

"What is wrong with Yesterday?"

Her eyebrows rose.

"She is Roma, she has an untraceable childhood, she lived with a seditious commune and was christened a Catholic; she should not be in your church, let alone ingratiating herself with you."

I nodded.

"The perfect mole."

"Quiet," she said. "I am glad you have seen sense."

I finished my cider.

"I will not use dead letter communication," I said softly.

'I will damn well choose who I have as a friend, and you can try filing for divorce, but I doubt you could even get a temporary annulment. You may think I am a small cog, but you are only a carrier pigeon, and any good soldier carries more than one in case the first one gets shot."

Having finished on an obscure metaphor I got up and walked away. However, I was acquiring a problem because my current major search would soon be finished, and I needed a channel to get the results home. I had an emergency fallback in case my handler got run over by a bus, or worse, but it was for emergencies, not because we were not seeing eye to eye.

I was right, my major Search yielded one result the following morning, or rather one result three times, whereas my second search yielded nothing. I changed the parameters on that and set it running again and sat back to think. I knew who had probably wanted that search, but they used me to keep everything at arm's length and would not welcome a direct approach. I had no way of contacting Yvette because we had not established an agreed protocol, which all meant I was up a creek without a paddle. However, I did have two options left and, ignoring the nuclear option, metaphorically ran up the red flag by going to my local library and using one of their computers to log onto a popular genealogy site and request a search for Victoria Hedegaard of Norwich, who had a child called Aloysius Murphy and a sister called Maude. The search came back with no results, but I hoped upon hope that the system worked as I had a football match to attend.

Carrow Road Stadium was heaving with people as it was the annual local charity match with Ipswich Town under 21s and Norwich under 21s. I endured the first half and found a pie and coffee stall where I bought a beef pie and a cup of coffee. One thing about Carrow Road is that even the stalls sell good quality food. Five minutes before the start of the second half I wandered outside to find a silver Jaguar and I slipped into the back. The guy in front wearing a leather Trilby hat did not turn round and I noticed that the two mirrors in the front had been tilted upwards.

"A man can die but once," he said.

"Nothing will come of nothing," I replied.

"I cannot command winds and weather.," he added.

"Desperate affairs require desperate measures," I responded.

He nodded.

"You have a problem?" He said in perfect BBC English.

"My new handler is being difficult, and we have not established any protocols, but I have hot goods and nowhere to pass them on," I murmured. "Too hot to be a dead letter."

"Have an early breakfast tomorrow," he said. "You might meet a doctor before surgery."

I climbed out of the car and walked back into the stadium. Protocol said I had to stay until the final whistle, and for once I observed protocol.

Drop

The Harbour View Café is at the lower end of the market, specialising in ultra-greasy fry-ups and cholesterol-inducing portions. I opted for a toasted crispy bacon sandwich and a mug of something resembling strong tea. She was wearing jeans, boots, and a grey parka and sat hunched over a croissant that looked as hard as iron. I sat down with my fare and bit into the sandwich; at least the semi-stale bread soaked up most of the fat.

"Anomalies bug me," I said.

"If you can fake sincerity, you can fake pretty much anything," she replied through gritted teeth.

She did not wait for the second bunch of doctor-orientated quotes.

"There was no need to call out the cavalry," she hissed.

"You left me high and dry, and I need a reliable contact, not a prima donna," I hissed back.

"Who's calling who a prima donna?" she snapped.

"Oh, this is hopeless," I groaned.

She held up a hand.

"Use Facebook and we'll meet at the viewing point, fallback to the Plaza. No dead letters"

I sighed with relief. She sat back.

"This is just disgusting."

I offered her a pear.

"She has two years off the grid, she left her commune

and disappeared for two years, that is not normal, and we have no idea how she got into this country in the first place; you are running into danger," she almost spat.

"Clean the palette," I said, holding out the pear.

She snatched it and stormed out. Protocol demanded that I stay and finish breakfast, but sometimes protocol is best ignored for health reasons.

Being out of pears I stopped off at Green's Greens, the grocery shop almost at the end of South Boulevard. Yaz was wearing light grey dungarees over a faded red top and wearing a belt bag. I watched her serve an elderly customer with an economy of movement, even packing her goods into her pull-along trolly after taking the money. I offered her my half a dozen pears, two apples and a punnet of early strawberries. Her eyes swing around.

"They are tasteless, we only stock them because Gordon's brother grows them."

I nodded and put them back on the shelf as she weighed and priced my purchases.

"Still on for tomorrow night?" I said casually as I tendered her a £10 note.

She grinned.

"Of course."

She leant towards me.

"There was a man here yesterday, he said he recognised me from Rouen, and he spoke to me in bad French, but he said I worked at a market stall, and I never worked in the market there. I told him it was a bad chat-up line, and I wasn't interested, and he went away. You are not checking up on me, are you?"

"What did he look like?"

"Tall, pale blue eyes, but they had a yellow tinge, he wore a green baseball cap and he stank of cigarettes."

I smiled, but I did not know him.

"I promise you that it is not me, I trust you otherwise I would not have shown you…"

I stopped because an old codger staggered in using two walking sticks. She nodded.

"Tomorrow, I will have eaten," she whispered.

I went home, got out the Social Services file and knocked off about six family maintenance dodgers. Sometimes it happens like that, other days you do not find one. However, I wanted to keep my hand in, just in case Yvette ever did manage to 'divorce' me. I was just about to go upstairs when my Playbook pinged up a result on my new deep search. This either meant I had tabled the various databases in the correct order, I was supremely lucky, or I'd picked up a red herring. However, with this type of search, I did not know who I was looking for, so the name meant nothing to me. I checked the clock and rushed down to the library to log onto a Facebook account that was not mine and make a comment on the top item including the words 'serene' and 'deadly.'

Wednesday morning, we met at our prescribed meeting place, the viewing point. She walked past with a small dog and then came over to sit down. I opened my mouth and she huffed.

"Let's cut the quotation interchange crap, I know who you are, and you know me."

I wondered if this was a test.

"You could be a body double," I said with a smile. "This mission is too important for me to allow you to jeopardize it."

She sighed.

"Well, it's just for the past two weeks there have been some extremely odd things happening at Clavius."

I grinned.

"Who chooses these quotes, they are always science fiction?" she muttered.

She closed her eyes.

"You called for a meet."

I took an apple out of my pocket and bit into it.

"Running a Lilac class search, that means results must be signalled within 24 hours. I have an initial unverified result."

She groaned.

"They let you loose on Lilac searches?"

"And several other shades of purple."

She gritted her teeth.

"I was never told that."

I checked the lie of the land.

"Have you called out the attack dogs on Yesterday?"

"In my position wouldn't you!" She exploded.

I held up a hand before she could say any more.

"To be honest, I would. If I find out anything about her past that I think you should know, I will tell you. Tell me about this seditious commune."

She sniffed.

"It was attached to the Convent of St Lydia and supposedly a place for the lost, the lonely and the dispossessed, but that meant all sorts of riff-raff passed through their hands."

I laughed.

"You are calling a convent seditious? I think your prejudice is starting to show."

I rummaged in my small cross-body bag.

"The book you wanted to borrow."

She took it, placed it in her bag and continued walking the dog. I went to the library to look up the Convent of St Lydia.

Just Hockey?

She turned up at 7:15 wearing a dark red midi-length red dress, red earrings, high-heels and wearing make-up. She was either seriously supporting her hockey team, or had other things in mind, but I couldn't throw stones because I had a new blue shirt, freshly dry-cleaned grey trousers, and freshly washed hair. We went straight into the TV room and settled down. She gazed at the TV screen that was just showing AllSport's Logo.

"Call me paranoid, but I would swear that someone has been through my things, Rene said much the same thing as someone had been through her bookcase, but that could be her current boyfriend as he is a…"

She took a breath.

"Am I safe?"

I held her hand.

"Quite safe, and if anything is happening, and it might not be, it is about me, not you."

She swallowed.

"You are a spook."

"I am a guy who does data searches to order, nothing more, nothing less, but my equipment is worth many thousands of pounds so I must be careful."

She glanced at me.

"One question; are you a terrorist target?"

"Not that I know of, they have many more important people than me to blow up."

I felt her relax and decided now was not the time to tell her that I had a Mossberg short-barrelled semi-automatic shotgun stashed behind my hot water tank and a 9mm pistol hidden inside my second exit from the basement. Fortunately, the logo on the screen dissolved, and we were looking at an ice hockey rink.

"That is not the same rink," I said.

She grinned.

"It is the O2 arena in Prague, I have not been there, but it is famous for being large."

"And the match is?"

"Bulgaria v Germany. Germany is the stronger team I think, but they have some prima-donnas who might not play with the team moves and are causing rivalries within the squad. That is our only hope."

The sound suddenly came on and all talking ceased as the announcers talked us through the teams; I must admit with the teams only having a few players on the rink I did not realise that you could have over twenty players a side.

We watched two fifteen-minute periods, and I could see what she meant. When certain players were on, they went for dribbling the puck rather than passing it, and even swiping it at the goal from a ridiculous distance. During the second break, I nipped into the kitchen and brought back two pasties and two glasses of Hibernal,

Seyval Blanc white wine.

"You are spoiling me," she said.

"You are worth spoiling," I replied smugly.

She studied the pasty.

"I have gone to ice hockey in Leeds, but they had beef pies with a thick crust."

"These are traditional Cornish pasties, but not from Cornwall."

She broke hers in half, and steam poured out.

"Suitably hot for keeping warm while sitting by an ice rink," I remarked.

She smiled gently, but I am not sure she got the joke.

It got to five minutes before the end and the score was 7-6 to Bulgaria, but Germany was pressing hard and showing their superior skills. I was sincerely hoping that there would not be a penalty shoot-out when one German player accidentally fell over another in Poland's goalmouth as they were crowding for a goal. Without warning two of the German players started fighting and rolling on the ground before standing up and wielding their sticks like clubs. The referee stood undecided for a moment and then sent them both off. Poland had a field day and finished 10-6. Yaz visibly sighed with relief as the final klaxon sounded.

"Good match?" I asked.

She smiled.

"One with the best result," she replied as she stretched.

"Cup of cocoa?" I ventured.

"Tea," she sighed. "Unless you have Horlicks. I had never tasted it until I came here, but now I have a liking for it."

I opened my mouth, but she put a finger to my lips.

"I will tell you my life's pilgrimage, but not tonight, I am still buzzing with a deserved victory."

She suddenly blinked, pointed at the TV screen, and laughed.

"The Germans have posted a formal complaint, saying that their team members were not fighting the opposing team."

"Will it stand?" I asked.

"Fat chance," she said. "Fighting is fighting and the referee's decision is final."

Ten seconds later a screen appeared saying that the appeal had been denied before metamorphosising into the AllSports logo.

For a moment we stood facing each other then she moved towards me and gave me a gentle kiss on the lips. The kiss turned into a cuddle and then more kissing until she just put her head to the side of mine and sighed. A few seconds later we parted, and I took her into the lounge while I made some tea, and we ended up side-by-side on my large settee.

"We must be careful," she said. "I do not want to run into danger."

"Danger?" I croaked.

She nodded and I liked the way her earrings swayed back and forth.

"I've made mistakes before," she said softly. "But I want us to do things properly, not have some one-night stand or a passionate affair; I want to know if it is love."

I sighed with relief because I thought she was going to say goodbye.

"I can live with that," I murmured.

I thought for a moment.

"Can I officially say that we are an item?"

She giggled.

"Oh yes, it's taken nearly a year to get you to notice me, but as they say, love the dog and you catch the man."

"I don't have a dog," I said, slightly bewildered.

She put her arm through mine.

"Oh yes you do, but it is called a sound system. You stroke it into life, you pat it when it behaves, you calm it when it yowls, and you feed it with contact cleaning fluid and lots of care. I am told you even stopped the church council from giving it euthanasia."

I chuckled.

"They allocated £15,000 for a new sound system, but at the same meeting worried that we might not have enough funds to keep our two parish nurses running; it was a no-brainer as they are more important to the community than my sound system."

She nodded.

"And a new dog might not be the same, it may be stand-offish and disobedient and respond to other people."

I laughed.

"You are barking mad."

"Barking," she mused. "You are getting the idea."

After I had taken her home and found out that my Honda Ridgeline might be comfortable and safe, but it was virtually impossible to lean over to kiss goodnight in, I went home and put the news on. The first item was that the police had arrested a man called Charlie Cowdry, and the shaky video showed a string of armed police smashing their way into his townhouse through the front window as the door was reinforced. The shot went back to the announcer who said dryly that the police had found bomb-making equipment and three assault rifles, but were wary of venturing into the attic without the bomb squad. I sat down and felt slightly sick, as that was the name and address I had passed on via Yvette. It rather brought home exactly what I was doing.

Work and more work

Thursday and Friday I dedicated to finding maintenance miscreants, setting a minor search in motion to track down a double defaulter and concentrating on those who had not paid for over eighteen months. I found nine alive, one deceased and one happily bigamously married in Bangor. My deep search ground on, yielding no more results, but taking longer than I expected, and my secondary search, another police search was still yielding no results and I was beginning to wonder is my prey had left Europe all together. However, one thing was becoming interesting, and that was The Convent of St Lydia as it was full of militant nuns. Not militant as in favouring confrontational or violent methods, but militant in terms of literary action about climate change, ecology, and declining communities as they wrote letters, lots of letters. If the articles I found about them were right, they had written multiple times to every MP, heads of oil companies, airline magnates, foreign ambassadors and just about anybody they thought would listen or not listen. As far as I could tell, they were not just lobbying, they were asking difficult, well-informed questions and posting these questions on social media. They did not blockade oil companies, but they sure blocked up their inboxes because they have a website encouraging others to write, or call, or email; basically, they were a thorn in the side of an awful lot of people, but I would hardly have termed them 'seditious.'

Dinner

Friday evening, I took Yaz out for our first evening meal together, and I chose Bladon Grange for the occasion as it is unpretentious, serves good food, and wouldn't break the bank. The restaurant is a large square with windows on three sides, one of which overlooks their lake and fountain. Unfortunately, I had booked late, and we had to sit on the other side overlooking their herb garden. However, I knew it was a mistake as soon as we entered the restaurant for sitting in a window seat overlooking the fountain was Yvette and another woman, who I vaguely recognised. As the maître d led us through the maze of tables I studiously avoided making eye contact with her, but I could feel her eyes on my back as Yaz, back in her red dress, walked in front of me. We settled down facing each other and I noticed a small curving scar on her right cheek and just how deep brown her eyes were as I could hardly see the pupils in the subdued lighting.

"You bring all your girls here?" She asked sweetly.

I swallowed and she tittered.

"You brought Rhona here, she told me, it is where she walked out on you because you asked if she still loved Bob and she thought it was insulting."

She reached across the table and held my hand.

"You can ask me anything, and I will not find it insulting; there can be no secrets between us." She hesitated. "Except for your work as I honestly do not wish to know."

She let go and I sighed.

"And she did still love Bob because she is back with him," I remarked.

Yaz grinned.

"She suffers from strawberries."

I blinked.

"Strawberries?" I echoed.

"When I lived with some nuns, Sister Anne was allergic to Strawberries, but she loved them so much that every Wimbledon she would hope the allergy had gone away, eat them and come out in a rash. Rhona loves Bob, or the idea of being with Bob, but she cannot stay with him because she prefers the idea to the reality."

"That is very profound," I said.

She laughed.

"It is what she told me; she can dream of being with Bob, but actually being with him turns always it into a nightmare."

Fortunately, I did not have to answer as our waiter brought over the menus.

The waiter, a solemn face man asked us if we wanted a drink in a somewhat thick French accent. To my utter surprise, Yaz spoke to him in French and his face lit up as they chatted away. It was interesting as she did not just speak French, she had the body actions to go with it and she was obviously quite fluent. Eventually, we asked for some white wine, and he wandered away.

"You had him eating out of your hand," I remarked.

"He is just a bit disorientated; he is over here on some sort of placement as the company that owns this place is French, but he says it is food, but not as he knows it."

I nodded.

"Your French is very good."

She gave a sweet smile.

"I lived there for a few years in a French convent so French was mandatory. What do you think the cheese-stuffed mushrooms will be like?" She added.

We ordered me in English and Yaz in French and then sat looking at one another as I had suddenly dried up. I did not want to appear prying, but I did not want trivial small talk. She suddenly smiled.

"I was brought up in a Romani camp, but it wasn't pure Romani as we also had a number of travellers from other communities. It was just normal life for me until mother left and Chantelle arrived with her daughter Tatti in tow, after that I found it chaotic and frightening at times. Weekends could be extra difficult because sometimes there were group barbeques, or even rival barbeques, and wine, beer, and illicitly distilled spirits, including a group of older teenage boys who believe that they had a divine right to do what they wanted, when they wanted." She shuddered. "They were the travellers, not the Romani boys, they knew their place. When that sort of thing happened, the only place of safety was on the top of a caravan. I used to climb up as soon as I could after eating." She paused. "Then just after I was thirteen I had to climb on a different large caravan as our was hosting the barbeque, the caravan skylight was open and as I lay there I heard Chantelle talking to one of her cronies and saying that now I was thirteen, next time we met her original group of Romani, she would palm me off on one of her cousins who was a widow with children. Next time she and father were both out, I stole her secret stash of money, believe me nothing is secret in a caravan, and set out for London."

"London?" I said in awe, "how did you hope to get to London?"

She raised her hands and shook her head.

"I was naïve, and the one thing mother had left under my pillow was a bright shiny UK passport. I caught a bus to Sofia and then a coach to Paris, from there I thought it would be easy to get a coach to London, but it all went pear shaped right at the start, because when I boarded the coach, it was full of young men going to a football match in Zagreb and tanking up on beer and rough vodka."

At that moment our cheese stuffed portobello

mushrooms arrived and she paused to eat.

They were delicious, but I had to wait for her to finish eating.

"You were on a coach full of football hooligans," I said dryly.

She smiled.

"Among all the men, halfway down the coach there was a nun sitting all alone, so I judged that I'd be marginally safer if I sat next to her. We got talking and I found out that she was Sister Jael and had been home to a family funeral and was going back to her convent in Rouen. Eventually I told her my story and then I slept on and off to Lyon because I had been too frightened to sleep at home." She took a sip of water. After Lyon she got all serious and said that if I went to London, I'd get eaten alive and probably end up in a brothel, or worse. I think she thought London was full of barbarians. She said I'd be safer going with her to Rouen as they had a hostel attached to the convent run by some friars. By then I was so apprehensive about everything I agreed. I had thought I was streetwise, but I knew nothing but camp life."

A waitress came and cleared away the empty crockery and served the wine, by now I was fascinated. She smiled and resumed.

"When we got to the convent, she took me to see The

Mother Superior, they chatted in French for a long time, and I got the impression that she was not best pleased. However, Sister Jael told me that The Mother though the hostel completely unsuitable because of my age. However, she would let me stay within the convent walls on three conditions. One I had to attend the daily offices and observe the convent routine, she said it would be good for me to have some order in my life. Two I had to help in the kitchens in the mornings and Three I had to study." She swallowed. "I agreed because I could think of nothing else, and she asked her three octogenarian nuns to educate me."

She laughed.

"And I had to learn French, she called it the language of heaven. One of the oldies, called Sister Abigail, had been a teacher and she taught me French and made me read French literature. When she started, I could barely read and write Bulgarian, but she was patient and kind and very French. Sister Leah taught me maths and, as an aside, bookkeeping, and Sister Sarah taught me history, geography, and watercolour painting." She gave a grim smile. "They did not even have a TV when I first arrived, so in the evenings we played Scrabble. They had one Scrabble set with a mixture of letters and we played what we called Frarian Scrabble as Sister Leah was Bulgarian, so both Bulgarian and French words were allowed, but they were very strict, there was no slang, no swear words, definitely no Franglais and 'holy' words from the Missal scored an extra two points. I was there for three and a half years and by the time I left French was my natural language."

I swallowed.

"Did you have to attend the services?"

She nodded.

"Lauds at dawn and Prime at sunrise, but the Mother gave me a dispensation on them, after that it was Terce mid-morning, sext at noon, None mid-afternoon, Vespers at sunset, and Compline before we all had to retire to our cells. The Mother Superior was right, I found it all daunting at first and had a period of resenting their intrusion into my life, but after six months it became a familiar and stabilizing pattern of life. After a couple of years, I started attending Prime, but I only made Lauds on my very last day. The liturgy seeps into the soul and I was confirmed when I was fifteen with Sister Jael sponsoring me and Sisters Anna and Leah as my Godmothers."

She stopped as our main meals arrived, chicken Caesar salad for her and mackerel salad for me.

"Why did you leave?" I asked.

She added a little vinegar to her salad.

"We had a new Mother Superior and she said it would be inappropriate for me to live in the convent after I was sixteen if I did not intend to become a nun. She was very kind, but she was very firm as she then told me that she would not accept me as a postulant as I needed some life experience first. She also pointed out that my UK passport would be expiring soon and if I, was going to go to England, now was the best time. She commissioned Sister Ruth who came from Canada to give me a crash course in English, and I left five months later the day before my sixteenth birthday." She swallowed. "I have to say that those nuns loved me into a normal life, but Mother was right as I'd only ever left the convent to go to the market."

She picked up her knife and fork and paused.

"What about you? What was your childhood like?"

I smiled, but in all that I had learnt something she may not have realised. Children's passports are issued for five years, so there was no way she could have had a ten-year passport, ergo it was false I just hoped that her story wasn't.

Memories

I was halfway through my salad, just at the point where you wonder if it is multiplying on the plate, when I got my thoughts together, as I do not like talking about myself.

"I don't remember much about primary school, except I made one good friend, Irah. We met at nursery school and somehow just drifted together. Her family owned an Asian delicatessen just down the road from me and our parents took turns in walking us to school." I paused because even now it was difficult. "When we were ten, we moved to a middle school for two years, and in the summer holiday before we went to senior school, her family went back to visit family in Pakistan, but I started senior school alone. To be honest, I worried that they had left her in Pakistan as one hears such terrible tales, but I was wrong. After a week I called at the delicatessen and found it shut. I knocked round the back and her mother, Tekia, opened the door and let me inside. She sat me down, gave me a drink of lemonade and showed me pictures of Irah's funeral and that of her father. He had taken her on a motorbike ride, but as a lorry overtook them, the front tyre blew out, the lorry swerved, knocked them off their bike and then ran over them with the back wheels. After that Tekia's flat over the shop became my second home as I was worried about her and tried to help her with the bureaucracy surrounding their shop. Then, one fatal week, she just gave up and committed suicide. She left me a letter thanking me for being a friend to Irah and supporting her but saying that she had nothing left to live for."

I paused and ate some more salad, Yaz did not say one word.

I decided to finish my schoolyear tales.

"After Irah's death, there was no joy at school until one of the math's teachers started a ham radio club, which expanded into a computer club. I guess I decided that making deep friendships was risky and became the pupil that spent time coding over lunch and being a bit of a nerd. It was the same at university, I had acquaintances, but not friends. Then one day I saw a poster in the Physics department corridor, it said 'You may understand the meaning of the universe, but do you understand the meaning of life?" It was a discussion group led by the university chaplain and it did two things for me. It introduced me to God, and it put me in a group where I could make friends. I still concentrated on software programming, but I had found peace. When I finished my BSc in computer science, I stayed on and did a one-year master's degree in data management." I glanced at her; she was still listening. "In most universities, there is what is called the milk round, where big firms come and put on displays and try to tempt you into their grubby hands., but I missed a lot of the talks as I was finishing my thesis. However, I was invited to the careers office and introduced to a tall chap and an elderly woman. They did not give me their names, but they did invite me to join the government's intelligence service with the promise of being able to play with big computers and sift data I could only dream of."

She smiled.

"So, you sold your soul."

I shook my head.

"I sought, and got, assurances. It would not be directly for the military; it would not be for arms development; and it would not be to subvert foreign government. I have been with them, or sister services, ever since."

She sighed.

"Enough history for one day, is it true our vicar one drove a bobsleigh?"

I smiled.

"Oh yes, but not for us, for Scotland."

We chatted about a few things, and I noticed out of the corner of my eye, a man sitting down opposite Yvette. Fortunately, I could get a good view of them in the end window and my blood ran cold. The man who had joined them was always referred to as 'The Major' and he had had the final say in recruiting me, but my blood ran cold because the woman he was sitting next to was obviously his daughter. They had the same lobeless ears, the same short noses, the same eyebrow line, and the same jawline. If Yvette knew him and her socially, I could be in big trouble if I took her on. Suddenly Yaz kicked me.

"You are spooking," she chided. 'You keep looking behind me."

I gave a weak smile.

"Sorry, someone I thought I knew, but I was wrong." I tried for a smile. "Does that ever happen to you; you see someone and think 'That is old Harry or Esmerelda the bell ringer."

She laughed.

"I have read The Hunchback of Notre Dame and Esmerelda never rang the bells, and no I have never met anyone from my old life. I have written to my father because the nuns at Rouen said I should make my peace with him and Chantelle, but I have only had a postcard back saying that I am his daughter and he understood why I left."

We finished and ordered our desserts. She finished her second glass of wine, not that I was counting, but I was determined to stick to one because I was driving.

"How did you meet your housemates Rene and Clair,"

I ventured.

She rocked her head from side to side.

"Via the Internet, how else? They put an advert on the local Facebook page saying they needed a housemate to share the costs, the cooking, and the domestics. I believe six people responded, but they chose me because they said I was normal."

"How little they know," I murmured.

We took coffee in a small lounge where there were magazines spread out on a table and an ambience of genteel tranquillity, and we had the place to ourselves because most people moved into the main lounge, but our French waiter had shown us here. We sat side by side on a green leather settee that had been worn into the 'comfortable' stage. She sighed as she pressed down the centre of a cafetière.

"What would you do if you were not a spook?" She murmured.

I managed a smile.

"I am not a spook, but if I moved on, I guess I'd manage a data centre or write code for a mobile phone manufacturer."

She shuddered and I decided to turn the tables.

"And what would you do, if you didn't sell greengrocery?"

She handed me a coffee and sat back.

"I do not have a recognised education like you, but I would like to teach as there must be joy in seeing pupils blossom and grow."

"Don't do yourself down, you speak three languages," I replied, taking her hand.

"Four; the Roma have their own language called Rromani Ćhib or sometimes just Roma. My father is only at home speaking that, although he also knows a fair bit of Bulgarian as he usually tries to find work in garages when we parked up." She put her head on one side. "Some of the travelling community who were with us occasionally bought and sold cars, but he would never work with them and called them 'gunoi,' which loosely translates as 'scum.'"

She put her arm through mine and leaned against me.

"This is a good place you have brought me to," she sighed.

Half an hour later I went to the gent's toilet in the basement. As I left the Major emerged from the shadows and took me to an empty clothes' storage area. "I have been told you are keeping dubious company, is that her?"

I nodded, quite overcome by his stealthy approach.

"Walk with care my friend," he said softly. "All those entrapment tutorials you watched are not just poppycock."

"I guess Yvette has been moaning," I groaned.

His eyebrows rose.

"Yvette?"

"You and your daughter are dining with her."

His eyebrows rose.

"You call her Yvette? Are you saying that she is now your cut-out?"

I sensed danger.

"Not my choice, but we are learning to get along, and she is only doing her job."

He suddenly smiled.

"I know nothing from her as she has not spoken to me about you; it is just a friendly warning. For your own sake, do a search on her."

"I'd need…" I blabbered.

"I am telling you to," he hissed. "Put your own mind at rest; do not rely on others."

He slunk away, for such a large man he made very little noise and I'd swear he'd managed to shrink his own shadow.

It occurred to me halfway up the stairs, that if Yvette had not talked to him, who had?

Hoping not to Find

Finding people about whom you have information is one thing but finding information about people you know is quite another. Fortunately, I knew her full name and date of birth as I had helped her fill in her church safeguarding form; if there was one thing about St Jude's, it was hot on safeguarding and even though you worked in a cage and moved little levers, you still needed a safeguarding certificate. However, I still sat for a good half an hour staring at my large monitor formulating where I would start. The main problem was that I had no access to any Bulgarian databases. I could access European ones, an extensive range of French ones, and, by a political quirk, a goodly number of Romanian ones, but the lack of Bulgarian ones could be a problem. However, there were always Bulgarian newspapers so at least with them and knowing that she had been in Rouen, I had a starting point. I wrote a routine and set it off my stack of mini-Macs on the search, it told me it would take 21 days, but I hoped it would turn up neutral information on the way. I analysed my feelings and decided that for one in my life, I hoped to find nothing of interest.

Later, I checked the UK passport register, and as I half-expected, she was not there, I also suspected that as she was Romani, they might not have registered her birth anywhere, but I was wrong because after 14 minutes I got my first result; her birth had been registered in Bucharest, which meant I now had the name of her mother, Maria Jean Roberts, but the father was not listed. I checked, and her mother was not and never had been, a UK passport holder either. I set one of my laptops doing a short search for her but somehow knew I was wasting my time.

I was wrong again as at 3 pm my laptop coughed up a birth registration in Lincoln for a Maria Jean Roberts. The mother was Jean Maria O'Conner and listed as Irish, and the father Joshua, Samuel Styles was listed as British. However, there was no address as the form showed 'No fixed abode – Travelling Community.' To my utter surprise, it also coughed up a death certificate for the father a month before the birth but registered in Alnwick, which made no sense whatsoever. However, there was one piece of good news here, because now I could probably prove that Yaz had an Irish grandmother and she would therefore be entitled to an Irish passport, which was a good fallback should she need it, provided of course that I could find an appropriate Irish Birth certificate for Jean O'Conner.

Sunday morning, I checked, but none of my searches had found anything new, which was a relief for my search into Yaz's background.

Yaz turned up five minutes before the service started looking flustered. She muttered something about oversleeping but was in position when the service started. I managed to suppress a taxi message halfway through the sermon and the vicar's radio mike died ten seconds after she had given the final blessing; otherwise, all went well.

"No alarm clock?" I murmured.

She huffed.

"It was late shopping night last night and we stayed open until 9 pm and then had to clear away. I must admit I thought the boss was mad, but we were working flat out most of the time."

"I hope you got overtime," I quipped.

She rolled her eyes.

"In my sort of job, you must be joking, but he did pay me until 9:45."

She disappeared to get the coffees while I started checking the earthing until our vicar, Vera, loomed large.

"Sorry," she said. "I forgot to turn the charger on and I was using it yesterday for a wedding rehearsal."

She gave her disconcerting smile.

"I have a wedding here next Saturday and the groom's

brother has a band which is going to play during the service. I showed them our sound system and they howled with laughter, The groom called it antediluvian, is it really that bad?"

I managed a smile.

"It does what we need, that's all that matters. There are better things for us to spend our money on."

She nodded.

"But if you got run over by a bus…"

I grinned.

"It is so old the Piltdown Man could maintain it."

She laughed and I relaxed.

"George is retiring as churchwarden," she purred. "Everybody knows he is the figurehead, but you do all the background work. Fancy regularising it."

I shook my head.

"I will assist, but I do not want a formal position."

She sighed.

"I feared as much."

She turned to go, sidestepped Yaz and set off like a guided missile towards Barbara.

Yaz put the coffee down.

"Is that a spook thing, keeping a low profile, or a personal thing?" She murmured.

"Personal, I do not like being on committees," I said truthfully.

She sat down.

"Neither do I, I always feel that other members think that 'she's just a greengrocer assistant, so what does she know?'"

"Probably more than them. If I know anything about Christianity, it is that we are all equal and all floundering our way through our life's pilgrimage." I replied.

I picked up my coffee.

"Can I entice my fellow traveller to lunch?"

She shrugged.

"Not today, our landlord is inspecting his property tomorrow and we are going to do a deep clean all round. It's not that the place is grubby, just lived it, but it needs to be shipshape." She flashed a smile.

"But Monday evening, after work, I shall be as free as a bird."

When I got home there were two more results on Yaz's search. She'd opened a bank account in Attleborough when she was eighteen and gained a National Insurance number when she was sixteen. After a bit of digging, I found her NHS number, but I do not have access to any NHS databases, so that trail ended there.

However, I received another message from a supposed online website; Yvette was back in town.

It Was on A Monday Morning

Monday there was a brisk wind, and she was sitting at her favourite table wearing a stylish blue coat. I sat down at the table.

"Ever felt that you could be 'chasing an untamed ornithoid without cause?'" I mused.

She rolled her eyes.

"Perhaps my 'mental pathways have become accustomed to your sensory input patterns."

I sat back.

"Enjoy your meal on Friday?"

She glanced around and leant forward.

"This is not a social call. We are going to be joined by two people, Captain Poldark from Military Intelligence and Ms Esmerelda Unthank from MI5. I have checked and counter-checked their credentials and The Major has sanctioned the meet. Once they have established contact, I am instructed to withdraw."

I swallowed.

"Not too far, I want you to maintain eye contact. Regardless of what they say, I will not leave with them, so if all three of us move together, I am in trouble."

She briefly smiled.

"But I am just a carrier pigeon. What do you expect me to do, poo on them?"

She raised a hand.

"I get the message, and the Major doesn't like it either,

so I am not alone."

She looked over my shoulder and smiled.

"Well hello again."

They sat down. He looked sun-tanned, alert, and dangerous as he had that military 'waiting for action' look about him, his eyes were also disconcerting, one watery-blue and the other grey. She was in a black overcoat that could have hidden anything, with shoulder-length blonde/greying hair and iridium blue eyes, but she could have been wearing contact lenses.

"What about the forests? You don't think anyone should care about these forests? What's going to happen if these forests and all this incredible beauty is lost for all time?" He said in a clipped Oxford accent.

"It calls back a time when there were flowers all over the Earth. And there were valleys. And there were plains of tall, green grass that you could lie down in... that you could go to sleep in," she added in a Sunderland accent that seemed false.

"And, there were blue skies, and there was fresh air, and there were things growing all over the place," I replied.

"Good film," remarked the Captain, "Silent Running."

"Not as good as Dark Star," I replied.

They looked at each other and mutually nodded. Yvette smiled and stood up.

"A gir's gotta go what a girls gotta do," she said in a

perfect Brooklyn accent before she walked away.

We sat looking at each other.

"I would like somewhere more private," she murmured.

"I wouldn't," I replied.

He leant slightly forward.

"We would like you to undertake a search for us, nothing special, but it could cover a large number of Government databases."

I managed to laugh.

"You must be joking; you have enough computing power between you to search every database on the entire planet faster than I can make a cup of tea."

"Not an option, not this time," she muttered.

I was hit by the blindingly obvious.

"You are looking for a mole, and if you do it, they will know."

The captain scowled.

"You don't need to know; we just need you to do it; an arm's length search and all that."

"How many databases and what size?" I asked.

"Many and large and on two continents, maybe three, correlating twenty-three ideas of search criteria but possibly generating others on the way. That's what you specialize in, isn't it? Searching while adding self-analysed criteria to widen or narrow the search."

I was surprised he thought he knew how I worked.

"Do I get a name?"

She shook her head.

"We do not want accusations off…"

She stopped and smiled.

I shook my head.

"I don't have any free resource that size."

He looked at her and she sniffed.

"I have access to funds, buy some more," she suggested.

I laughed.

"I would need five computers at…"

She held up a hand.

"£20,000 enough? And you have four weeks max." She flashed a smile. "You could keep the equipment when finished."

I glanced at each of them.

"I have to eat; £30,000 for equipment and five weeks work. If I have to build a stack it takes time."

She ran her tongue around her mouth.

"£25,000."

I would have accepted, except the Captain held up his hand.

"This is not a horse trade. £10,000 and we supply you computing needs." He paused. "This is a double-red job, your security clearance will be amended appropriately."

I stared at him and wondered just how generous this bearing of gifts would be, especially as it would give me an indication of how worried they were.

"I'd need three brand new and untouched Apple Mac top of the-range enhanced Pro computers, a 24" iMac, an iPad Pro, some interface cables, and the activation costs for another fibre optic link. I have a six-strand fibre cable, but I am only using four."

I waited, my shopping list was around £25,000 without the fibre optic link and it was a good litmus test. He suddenly smiled and pulled out a book that he thrust at me.

"Forget Dark Star, read this, it will blow your mind."

"And I'll use my own handler," I said firmly. "She'll need to be briefed."

"We prefer our own," she said smoothly, letting her Sunderland accent slip a little.

"And I prefer mine, that way I know the chain of communication will not be interfered with."

"We are all on the same side," he muttered. "But in your position, I understand."

They got up and walked away, and I wondered just what I was letting myself in for.

Groundworks

It was nearly an hour before Yvette returned, during which time I had had a toasted teacake, and coffee and mentally considered how I would set up a large computer triumvirate and cope with the heat output because if I worked them hard, they would get quite warm. She arrived back and flopped down in the seat with a cappuccino. She looked a bit mystical.

"I have had a field promotion because my security rating has been upped with the Major's approval," she suddenly smiled. "I could do with the extra pay, but why?"

"Don't ask, just enjoy, but mug up on Shakespeare and Chaucer."

She groaned and I leant forward slightly.

"You got a gun in that bag of yours?"

"Standard issue .22 palm pistol."

I nodded.

"Get it replaced with a gun worthy of your new status, say a nice 9mm Springfield Armory Hellcat."

Her eyebrows rose.

"Same as mine," I murmured. "I hope to God that we never have to use them, but that pair have one hell of a problem and are throwing money at it. Money leaves trails and it could end with us."

She understood; I wanted her to watch my back.

"Yesterday," she hissed. "You will have to break it off

and break it off now!"

She was certainly single-minded.

"Have you found anything that indicates she is a terrorist?"

"I can find damn all, and that is what worries me," she snapped.

I passed her an apple, which as usual had an implanted MicroSD card.

"Parents and grandparents' names. She was also in a convent in Rouen from 13 to 16, which is why she speaks fluent French, or didn't you know?"

She stayed silent.

"We've got to work together. Investigate Yesterday if you must, but I'd like a deep search on those two goons. They look like their backs are against the wall and I do not want them lashing out and catching us in the process."

She nodded.

"The Major said the same, he doesn't mind inter-agency work, but those two are…"

She stopped and smiled, went to stand, and sat down.

"The restaurant; please tell me you will not investigate Camile."

"The Major's daughter?" I ventured.

She scowled.

"The Major's niece."

I shook my head.

"Not my job to investigate her, but if you are becoming more than just friends, you might want to; after all, that's what you expect me to do with Yesterday."

Mid-afternoon a Curry's delivery van turned up and I took delivery of a 'fridge-freezer.' Inside the box was all the computing equipment I had mentioned, plus a cover for the iPad with a built-in keyboard. Later a pizza delivery driver delivered an 8" pizza and in the box were the latest mid-size iPhone, and an Apple watch. The double red dot on the packaging told me that they had been modified to receive encrypted messages and I began to feel quite uneasy. Yaz had called me a spook, and this stuff was serious spooking equipment. An hour later I got a message from one of our own online pseudo-stores saying that they hoped I liked my new purchase and that it could revolutionise my daily life.

I had time before I met Yaz to take the covers off the large computers and check them over, despite the fact they were all factory wrapped and in sealed boxes. I didn't worry about the software because I would be stripping out most of the Apple software and installing a tailored version of Linux, but the hardware was another matter, but there was nothing I could spot so either they had modified all three computers, or not touched them, and I hoped it was the latter.

Just before I left the lights on my new modem started to flash and change colour, meaning tomorrow I could start linking everything up and dropping in my search programmes. Part of me liked the challenge, and another part was yelling 'Be careful,' but the die was cast.

Just Talking

When I got to the greengrocer she was just finishing packing up, that is bringing the outside display inside. She let me in the shop while she packed a carrier bag with some fruit and veg and set the alarm system.

"The wages are the bare minimum, but I do get as much fruit and veg as I like for personal use, it is my one and only perk," she murmured before she greeted me with a kiss.

She paused at the door.

"I know you said meal and cinema, but could we just go to yours and have a takeaway? I don't feel like a film tonight," she sighed on a downbeat note.

"Bad news?" I ventured.

She nodded.

"Our landlord didn't really want to do an inspection, he told Rene that he intends to sell the trailer and has given us the mandatory eight weeks' notice. I guess we should have seen it coming, but we were all wearing blinkers."

I tried to understand.

"Blinkers?"

She gave a wan smile.

"The site does not allow trailers that are more than fifteen years old, ours is twelve years old, so he wants to sell while he can. We all knew of this rule but hoped that we had another three years."

She perched against a bar stool.

"Things would have changed anyway as Clair is pregnant and trying to bring up a child in the trailer would have been a nightmare." I got the wan smile again. "I guess all good things come to an end and Rene has started house hunting."

She stood up and picked up her bag.

"So, some comfort food would be nice."

She stood still and I went over to hug her. In some ways I knew how she felt as when I woke up in hospital with two new knees, I knew that my days in my tall thin three-storey townhouse were over, fortunately, it was not mine, it was the company's, and together we made alternative arrangements.

She prepared a salad while I went to the best pizza shop in town and brought a 25cm pizza as they were Italian and shunned imperial measure. She had laid out the salad on two plates in the conservatory, so we cut off two large slices and left the rest in the oven to keep it hot. We ate in almost silence as we surveyed the view.

"Will the three of you stay together?" I asked.

She shook her head.

"Mother Sapphira told me that I should not be frightened of change as it did not mean things would automatically get worse as they could also get better. She said the way through change was to hang onto God's coattails, but that is easier said than done."

I tried to absorb this.

"Who was Mother Sapphira?

She gave her wan smile.

"The Mother who told me I could not stay at Rouen, but she had already made provisions. After my one and only Lauds, the other nuns all said goodbye and gave me a rosary and a silver cross on a chain."

She fiddled and brought out an inch-high cross from under her neckline.

"We had to start so early as Sister Deborah, who was my escort, and I rode in the back of a grocer's van to Bolbec and then on a bus to Fécamp. There we caught a yacht called The Sweet Sultana for a passage to Brighton; I think Mother Sapphira had called in some favours and the owner was a devout Catholic, who treated us like royalty. The journey took ten hours, and he fed us twice and encouraged us to sit on the deck and relax. Once at Brighton, we were met by Customs, who were not interested in Sister Deborah or me and just waved us on, but I am afraid they virtually took the poor chap's boat apart as they suspected he was drug-running. I know because Mother Sapphire wrote to me and said that he considered it an honour to suffer for the faith."

She nibbled a radish.

"Then we had a series of busses and coaches to the

Convent of St Lydia where Sister Deborah stayed for two days before going on to a convent in Glasgow."

She suddenly stood up and went to fetch some more pizza before it was shrivelled up.

"Were the convents the same?" I asked.

She laughed.

"Oh no, for a start it was an Anglican convent, but Mother Sapphira said that would be good for my soul, almost as if I was going over to the dark side. They had the same seven offices in the convent, but I was not in the convent and if I attended, I had to use the visitor's gallery and they were behind a wrought iron screen. They ran an organic market garden to the side of their convent, that had an old farmhouse where workers could stay. I was given a room in the attic, and I loved it because of the view. It was all done properly because the Mother Superior there liked order and clarity. I became an apprentice horticulturist and lived in a loose commune with eight other staff, but I ended up working in the office, not out in the beds, unless it was harvesting time for strawberries or apples or potatoes when it was all hands to the pumps. Daniel, who ran the place, sent me one day a week to learn computing, word processing and spreadsheets, the rest of the time I answered the phone, made his tea, and tried to keep track of sales, because the nuns gave some of the produce away, but were a little lax of saying where it went."

She bit her bottom lip.

"I guess I should have gone out with the others to clubs and gigs, but I stayed within the confines of the offices and gardens because I was afraid. This was not a nice, ordered life like in Rouen, people came and people went, only half went to Mass on Sunday and I felt that if they were giving me an apprenticeship, I ought to try and do my best." She closed her eyes. "And then Hugh Younger arrived as manager when Daniel moved on."

She ate some pizza and I waited.

She sighed.

"He swept me off my feet, I'd never had a proper boyfriend and he just overwhelmed me, and when I was eighteen, we left to run what we hoped to be a self-sustaining smallholding near Woodbridge in Suffolk. It was then I found out that the nuns had been paying me and saving the money and Sister Dahlia took me into town and opened a bank account for me and paid the money in. She also told me, in no uncertain terms, that it was my money and if Hugh wanted to spend his money on a pipedream I should keep my nest egg as an escape fund, at the time I thought she was bonkers, but she was right."

"Sister Dahlia?" I echoed.

She laughed.

"They were ecologically bonkers. The sisters all had flower names, Sister Buttercup, Sister Bluebell, Sister Rose, Sister Fuchsia, Sister Lilly, Sister Wisteria, and so on. They wouldn't have cut flowers in their chapel, but they had potted plants, and as far as they were concerned, running an organic market garden was not a lifestyle choice, it was a divine command." She sighed. "But they were good to me, twice."

"Twice?"

She nodded.

"I won't bore you with the details, but it didn't work out. I spent two years with Hugh on that smallholding and it ended up as a nightmare, not nirvana, which is what he called the place. In the end, I could never work hard enough to satisfy him, the food I cooked was always overdone or underdone and I ended up committing a cardinal sin in his eyes; I became pregnant. He told me, in no uncertain terms, that the timing was wrong, and I should terminate the pregnancy as the small holding would sustain two, but not three if I could not work full time. That's when I left him and realised that I had nowhere to go. I had not made any friends and knew nothing beyond the limits of our little farm. That's when I went back to the convent."

I swallowed.

"And the child?"

She shook her head and started to gently cry.

"She died inside me. I was thin, undernourished, wracked with chlamydia, and she was malformed from the start. I had a miscarriage at fifteen weeks, and it was the worst time of my life. There had been so much promise, but it ended on a bathroom floor. I called her Susanna, after the flower, and the nuns held a memorial service for me and buried the foetus in their own graveyard and gave me dispensation to visit even though it was on their side of the fence."

She looked at me as tears streamed down her face.

"Those nuns loved me back into life, without them I might have killed myself, but they showed me that life is worth living and that God walks beside us, even in the deepest grief."

I reached out and held her hand. I wanted to cuddle her, but holding hands made the emotional contact she needed.

After I took her home, I looked up Hugh Younger, he was easy to find because Yaz had not only given me his name but also the name of the smallholding, Nirvana. It looked like after she left, he tried to turn it into a commune, failed and worked for a market garden in Shropshire. Now he had a website extolling organic farming, but he also had a blog that showed he was anti-monarchist, anti-parliamentarian and anti-police while extolling the virtues of two despotic totalitarian states and advocating that all refugees should be sterilised on entry to prevent over-population. I knew that if Yvette found out this connection, and some of the conspiracy theories he was supporting, she would no doubt throw her rattle out of the pram, but I wasn't about to tell her until I had a plan to head her off.

Unhappy Memory Loss

Tuesday, I started stripping out some of the Apple operating system on my three computers and installing a special version of Linux. However, it was not straightforward; I checked on the free space on each machine and one had 26Mb less than the others. It took me over an hour to find an encrypted file masquerading as part of the system software and another twenty minutes to strip it out. I then checked the 24" iMac desktop computer and found the same piece of software, but I did not strip that out. Instead, I decided to redeploy an old iMac I was using as a personal machine to be the stack controller and took the new iMac upstairs to replace it. Even so, it was past midnight when I had all three of the new computers laced together and up and running well enough for me to set a couple of test routines running. Call me paranoid, but I did not want to leave any stone unturned, just in case more little nasties were lurking deep in the embedded software.

I got up late on Wednesday and found all my test routines had run without a hitch. However, I did have a different problem because my search on Yaz had listed all the nuns at St Lydia's and Sister Dahlia was not included. There was a Sister Daphne, but that was an almost impossible mistake to make. I searched the

Market Garden website and the local newspaper and struck paydirt because there was a letter to the editor in the local rag. The letter was moaning about the needless use of herbicides on verges, and it was signed by Sister Dahlia on behalf of the Convent of St Lydia.

As agreed, I turned up at 2 pm and found a pensive Yaz. She bit her bottom lip.

"I don't know what you had planned, but could you take me to Deopam in Norfolk, I'd like to visit Susanna, I haven't been for a while, and I would hate her to think I had forgotten her."

I nodded and we climbed in. She carefully laid a bunch of flowers on the back seat while I set the sat-nav and we set out.

"I am sorry if I have disturbed old memories," I said.

She shook her head.

"The memory is part of me, wasn't it Isaiah who said that a mother could never forget the child she has borne?"

I nodded, but most of the Old Testament was a bit of a mystery to me.

She closed her eyes, and I took a gamble.

"Would you like me just to shut up for a while?" I asked gently.

She nodded and I just drove as she say there with her eyes closed lost in her thoughts.

Deopam is not just rural, it feels like it has dropped off the map as there is nothing there except the red brick convent walls and the market garden on the other side of a small river. Yaz directed me to a lay-by close to a door in the wall. She checked her cheap watch and swallowed.

"I'd like to attend None with the sisters and then visit Susanna; I'll be about an hour, and I'll probably come out of a door in the convent wall just around the corner, it leads straight into their garden, but it normally locked."

I swallowed.

"Is there any chance I could…"

She shook her head, climbed out and went to the door I could see and pressed a brass bell push. A couple of minutes later she went inside.

I took a walk and had a look around the market garden. There was an old farmhouse, neatly arranged flower beds and a group of young people half a mile away hoeing a large vegetable bed.

"Can I help you?" said a soft Cornish voice and I turned round to see a tall brunette woman in a denim onesie holding a rake.

I decided on a frontal approach and showed her my ID card but did not give her my name.

"Used to be a guy here called Hugh, Hugh Younger, I'm just doing a bit of follow-up."

She chuckled and shook her head.

"Long gone."

"Did you know him?" I probed.

She sighed.

"Oh yes, he had a little commune in Suffolk, his vision was sound, but his interpretation was flawed."

I raised an eyebrow.

"Too much skunk that he grew at the back of one of the greenhouses, too much potato vodka from his illegal still in the barn and too much time online when he should have been working," she sighed. "In the end, he suffered a peasant's revolt."

"Peasant's revolt?" I echoed.

"The rest of us had a meeting and decided to leave en masse as we thought he had lost the plot. I came here, because he had mentioned it, and stayed to eventually become the manager."

I nodded.

"Did he ever mention a woman called Yaz?"

She huffed.

"He never mentioned anything about his past, he used to say "Yesterday is history, tomorrow is a mystery' as if it were some sort of golden mantra."

She looked up and frowned. I followed her view. The youths were now playing piggyback jousting. She took a small aerosol-driven horn off a shelf and sounded it. They waved and got back to work, and I took the opportunity to leave.

I found a small concrete hard standing near the second door and waited. Suddenly the door opened, and Yaz appeared and beckoned to me. I wandered over. She held her finger to her lips and leant forward.

"They are all inside, we have five minutes."

She took me around the edge of a pleasant lawned garden and through a wooden gate. Here there was a neat graveyard with twenty or so graves each with a neat wooden cross. She led me to a small plot in the corner by a tree. There were no dates on the small cross, just the words, 'Susanna, much loved.' Her bunch of flowers was lying at the foot of the cross. She blew a kiss, grabbed my hand, and took me outside. Just to the left of the door was a small wooden bench and was sat on it and I held her close as she buried her head into my shoulder.

"I was frightened beyond belief," she sobbed. "But I so wish she has lived."

We must have been there for ten minutes when a nun in a rough brown cape came out of the door and sat down beside Yaz.

"Sister Matthiola," Yaz murmured. "She taught me

plainsong. Sister this is Allan."

The woman smiled, but I could not determine her age, perhaps forty, perhaps older. She pushed her cowl back revealing greying brown hair that somehow matched her light brown eyes.

"Mother Matthiola," she murmured. "It is my turn to take up the reins for three years."

She smiled at me.

"None of us is above the others, but there is a necessity for a leader, so we rotate the dubious honour."

I noticed her holding Yaz's hand.

"You have joined a church?"

Yaz nodded.

"St Jude's at Eastburgh Point."

Her eyes moved to me.

"And do you go there?"

I nodded and felt like I was being assessed for suitability.

"And what do you do?"

"I work with computers," I responded.

She frowned a little.

"I fear that there is more to what you say than you are…"

Yaz squeezed her hand.

"I know what he does, the first time I went to his house he showed me. He searches for people who want to hide because they are shirking responsibilities or are a danger to others. I do not want to know the details, but we have no secrets. I have been telling him about my life, and I have told him about Susanna," she said softly.

Mother Matthiola appeared to nod to herself.

"We have had three months of prayer and reflection to assess if we are achieving anything, or if we need to perhaps move into more online lobbying or perhaps stop. Sometimes it is good to stop and listen to God and not repeat the same old formulas."

She suddenly smiled.

"So, at the moment we are all in the chapel and will be so until four o'clock, so if you wished more time in our garden, you could have another fifteen minutes and disturb no one."

Yaz glanced and me and I nodded, so she dashed off through the gate leaving me with Mother Matthiola and the distinct feeling I was being set up.

A place in our hearts

Mother Matthiola sat quietly beside me as if somehow she was taking stock of me.

"We all feel we let Yesterday down, she came to us for sanctuary, and we introduced her to Hugh, who proved to be a total disaster for her," she eventually said in her funny English-but-not-English accent.

I managed a smile.

"She told me that you all loved her back to life, I think you have a deep place in her heart."

She didn't move.

"The question is, 'Does she have a deep place in your heart?' We failed her once and I would not like to think that we fail her a second time," she said softly.

I don't think anyone else could have asked me such a question, but she did it so gently as to make it acceptable.

"She is digging a place in my heart," I replied enigmatically.

Seditious nuns or not seditious nuns, I decided to take a gamble. I pulled out my ID card and showed it to her. It clearly stated that I was an authorized officer in British Intelligence. I swallowed.

"I am not a front-line officer, but the sorts of work we do can make us see shadows in bright sunlight and dark corners in radiantly lit rooms. I think you can understand that this can make relationships difficult as you must trust someone else to have a relationship. I am sure I am starting to do that with Yesterday. She has her past, and I have my job, but we are working it out."

Mother Matthiola gave a slight nod.

"Good, and do you believe in God?'

"Yes, but I'm a bit fuzzy around the edges."

She laughed.

"We are all fuzzy around the edges."

She stood up.

"Yesterday is precious to us; she is always welcome here," she said gently before heading for the gate.

She paused and came back, put her hand in her cape pocket and dropped a small wooden cross into my hand.

"Pray for us Allan as we try and pray for the world."

She looked out across the countryside as if seeing it for the first time and she seemed to start speaking to herself.

"Last week, we had a woman who claimed to be an ecologically minded reporter asking questions about why we do what we do, and the answer 'because God compels us to' did not seem to satisfy her. I think she is troubled deep down inside. I gave her a cross and told her to pray and trust in God. She had a string of black pearls, if you know her, tell her I will always talk to her." She turned and walked off through the little gate, she did not look back.

Yaz came out five minutes later looking more

composed. She sat down and held my hand.

"Mother Matthiola says that 'you'll do,'" she announced.
I smiled because she made it sound like a blessing straight from the Almighty.

"Did you ever consider being a nun?" I asked out of sheer curiosity.

She hesitated and then nodded.

"Not here, back in Rouen, but you have to be called to be a nun, and I am not called," she said forlornly. She squeezed my hand.

"And I am glad because if I was, I could not have you."
I sighed and we sat in the sun for a little more, until at some unseen command we both decided to leave.

Fortune shined on us as just outside Diss there was a KFC. We used the drive-through and I ordered chicken and chips twice with two coffees. In no time at all, we were sitting in the carpark eating our wares.

"Thank you," she said. "I needed that."

"We can get a KFC anytime," I quipped, and she punched me not too gently on the arm.

"You know what I mean. It is not only visiting Susanna, but it is also being able to sit in their garden and absorb God's peace. Life is turbulent, and I need to be able to grasp onto God's coattails."

I nodded and she flipped subjects to almost catch me off guard.

"Is what you do dangerous?"

I chose my words carefully.

"Not of itself and safety comes from lying low, blending in and being at arm's length. However, should I turn up a suspect who can trace that I know them and their whereabouts, it may not be so safe."

She chewed on her bun.

'I can handle a shotgun. Dad had an old Toz double-barrelled, and he taught me to use it when I was eleven, it had a fearsome recoil. We used to hunt rabbits, once Dad shot a goose, but he preferred to use snares."

I swallowed.

"I hope it never comes to that."

She sipped her coffee again and started to speak softly.

"I left when I was twenty-two. I knew then that I was not called to be a nun and needed to find a career. Sister Hosta had a brother who had a friend that ran a greengrocer and whose wife had just given birth to twins. He put in a word for me, and I moved to Eastburgh Point."

She finished her coffee and sat back.

"The pay is abysmal, and it is cold in the winter, but would it surprise you if I said I loved it? You meet the same people week in and week out, you get to know them. Last February we didn't see Mrs Greeves for ten days and Benny rang the social services. She was OK but had been told to have meals-on-wheels and it was taking all her pension, so she couldn't buy her usual fruit. Benny took a box round and gave her social worker hell for not realising the implications of what she had put in place. She still gets meals-on-wheels, but now it is subsidised so she can buy her bananas and easy-peelers again."

"Will you'll stay there?"

She grimaced.

"No, I've been taking evening classes in retail management, and I want to run a greengrocery or maybe a bakery, at least that would be warm in winter.

We finished our meal, and I collected the rubbish.

"Do you have ambitions, or are you content to stay as you are?" She mused.

I shuddered because she had asked the one question I kept asking myself.

"There are a million different jobs in IT, but I don't know how to manage large computer suites, run multi-access software packages, or get robots to move to my commands, so I am a bit limited. I have carved a niche for myself and, to be honest, don't know how to leave it." I hesitated, but she had told me her life story. "And I'm not sure I want to leave it."

She nodded.

"But you are not a free agent."

I nodded.

"But I get a decent salary, a decent pension and have a decent house." I closed my eyes. "And they stuck by me when I had my accident, they could have paid me off as I am supposed to have a certain degree of fitness."

She looked pensive.

"You are sure it was an accident?"

I swallowed and nodded because to think otherwise led to too many questions to formulate, let alone answer.

Routines

I spent eight hours writing routines and sub-routines, but with so many variables and such large and varied databases I kept adding IF-THAN-ELSE statements until I had them nested so deep, I wondered if any information would emerge. At four o'clock I made my way to the viewing point, Yvette was already there with a different dog by her feet.

"Patience is a conquering virtue," I sighed as my knees ached from sitting still for too long.

"People can die of mere imagination," she replied. "But if gold rusts, what then can iron do?"

"Amor vincit omnia," I replied.

"Did you have to choose Chaucer," she moaned. "He's so obtuse at times."

I smiled.

"That's the point."

She rolled her eyes.

"Why are we meeting?" She said tetchily.

I checked, but we were alone apart from an old lady three benches away and upwind, even so I turned away from her and spoke softly.

"I'd like you to do three things. Firstly, Yaz is being evicted from her trailer, is that the Major's doing? Secondly, the pair of spooks want me to search our own company database; is the Major happy with that? And finally, I want to know if there is a report on my accident and its conclusion?"

She groaned.

"Don't want much do you?"

I smiled as the old lady got up and tottered away.

I leant slightly closer.

"That old lady, she was here twice when I saw my previous contact, she needs checking out."

"Oh please!" She exclaimed. "She's been checked out; she lives in a home for the elderly two streets away."

I smiled.

"In that case, why is she here and not there having her tea?"

She nodded and tutted.

"Your woman, she still has two years missing, bookended by her time at St Lydia's. That's time enough to go to Russia or China or anywhere and be trained in insurrection."

"Or two years trying to live a self-sustainable life on a smallholding near Woodbridge called Nirvana. Since she was there, and I stress, since she was there, the chap running it, called Hugh Younger, has rather gone off the rails. I think he is a crackpot rather than a subversive, but it could be worth checking him out. He is now working in Shropshire."

She nodded and I took a gamble.

"And did you find out anything when you visited the St

Lydia convent beyond what we already know?"

She grimaced.

"Only that they are certifiable as I suffered a forty-minute lecture on the ecology of hedgerows and the necessity of not killing too many wasps."

"And Mother Matthiola says if every you want to talk, she has a confidential listening ear."

She scowled.

"You've been there?"

"Of course, and you stood out like a sore thumb because you did not take your pearls off."

She stood up.

"Tomorrow, noon at our other place," she commanded.

"At the fallback," I replied. "Let's not get too complacent, little old ladies might have big ears."

I waited ten minutes and then took a walk along the promenade and back, ending up at The Fairmile Inn. Inside it was not too crowded and I ordered a pint and a bowl of goulash and settled down to watch the rerun of T20 cricket being played in Japan for the first time. The Japanese team had some outstanding fast bowlers and showed magnificent prowess in slip catching, but their batting collapsed under the onslaught of spin bowling by our latest ball-curling maestro. There were rumours of a test match in two years' time and if they improved their batting they would be worthy opponents.

Friday morning, I checked and rechecked my coding, added a couple of extra sub-routines and loaded it all, plus my core search programmes, into my new stack. By mid-afternoon I was ready to go, but instead of pressing the 'run' button, I drove out to Wellcombe Lake and Sport's Centre. Here I parked in the carpark and idly walked around the towpath to sit on one of the benches overlooking the end of the open water swimming area and waited. She turned up with a medium sized Staffordshire Bull Terrier in tow and sat down.

"Vanity of vanities; all is vanity. What profit hath a man of all his labour which he taketh under the sun?" she said looking out over the lake and patting the dog.

"The wind goeth toward the south, and turneth about unto the north; it whirleth about continually, and the wind returneth again according to his circuits," I replied dutifully.

She wrinkled her nose.

"I can find nothing that implicates the Major in Yesterday's landlord's actions. However, £1000 in cash has been taken out of the slush fund and the landlord has just bought his son a new mountain bike, the retailer told me that he paid cash, but the two may not be connected."

She scratched the dog's ears.

"I asked the Major about you searching our database on behalf of a third party, and he said, 'over my dead body.'"

She glanced at me.

"I now have a full timeline for your Yesterday and she is probably clean, but I am still trying to track her movements before she went to France. Finally, there is a report on your accident and the conclusion was that it was not a deliberate action. The lad driving the fork-lift needed counselling and we could find no connections with any known miscreants. You were just unlucky."

She sighed.

"And out little old lady used to be a policewoman in Cairo, but according to the nursing home she lives in her own world and often forgets meals. However, last week she was out all night on Wednesday, so we are probing a little more."

I cleared my throat.

"Thank you, but where do you get the dogs?"

She smiled.

"I am trying to find the right dog for me and have been walking them for a local Blue Cross animal refuge, they are perfect cover because I am just a dog walker." She flashed a smile. "You ought to get one, better than any burglar alarm and a deterrent to any would be snoopers. They have a beautiful Koodle at the moment, it would be a good guard dog and perfect cover for you when out walking and meeting people."

I laughed.

"What the hell is a Koodle?"

She chuckled.

"Is a cross between a Hungarian Kuvasz and a standard poodle, it is ivory coloured and looks like a chunky poodle. I'm told it loves swimming in the sea, but its thick curly coat holds an awful lot of water, so stand clear when it shakes itself."

I frowned.

"Are you trying to order me to get a dog?"

Her eyebrows rose.

"I wouldn't be so presumptuous, but you can't be alert all the time and whatever alarm system you have; you know. and I know, it can be bypassed."

She stood up and walked off with the dog by her side and she was right, nobody in their right mind would try and physically attack her with a Staffie around, but like her pearls, it made her distinctive.

Impetuous

Later, I drove over to Yaz's trailer to find a tough looking woman loading bin-bags onto a small three-wheeled vehicle rather like a cut-down tuk-tuk. Yaz came out with another bag and piled it on before the woman started the small engine and pottered off.

"Rene and Clair have taken over another trailer on the other side of the site, it is the same size as this, but there will only be the two of them," she said, somewhat downbeat.

I put two and two together.

"They didn't invite you?"

She gazed at the tuk-tuk as it turned left.

"I didn't want them to; they want to bring up baby and I am not sure if I could cope."

I took her hand and she composed herself.

"Our landlord has given them a refund and told me I can stay for another two weeks, then he really should return our deposit."

"And then?"

She shrugged.

"Looking for another house-share and I have my name down for a studio flat in Marigold Housing; I am nearing the top of the list, but they are as rare as hen's teeth, and I can't afford a one-bedroom flat even though a couple are coming up soon."

We went inside and there were three more bin-bags

inside the door and a feeling of emptiness as two of the bedroom doors were open exposing bare beds and open wardrobe doors. I suddenly became irrationally annoyed at The Major, if he had caused this it was totally unwarranted.

"You could always share my house," I blurted out.

Her eyebrows rose.

"Just share the house?" She said menacingly.

"One day I hope to share our lives, but I'm not trying to pressurise you!" I blabbed.

She blinked.

"I am becoming English, I am making tea," she said turning round and walking off.

She plonked down a mug of tea in front of me as I wondered just how the three of them had managed in the small lounge. She sat down next to me on the small settee.

"Is this offer made out of pity?" She said acerbically.

I grabbed her hand.

"Not pity; affection. I hope that we can be more than just friends, but I know that you want to take it one step at a time. However, events are…" I blethered.

She huffed.

"The timing is wrong. With Hugh, before I knew what I was doing I was in a draughty cottage with no electricity and water from a hand pump in the kitchen.

With you I could be living in a warm and cosy bungalow with all mod cons and be sucked into a relationship out of convenience."

I nodded.

"Bad idea then, but wherever you move to I will…"

She squeezed my hand.

"I just need time to think, and so do you. Do you really want me around 24/7? Won't I get in the way of your spooking?"

I opened my mouth, but she ploughed on.

"And what when you are out? Will I be safe, you do not install a burglar alarm like yours, with CCTV and a security door on the basement for no reason."

I grasped at straws.

"Dog, I'm thinking of getting a decent sized dog."

She looked at me and then giggled, chuckled, chortled, and laughed.

"If you could see your face, you look like you are sucking coconut size lemons."

"He's at the Blue Cross, he's a koodle."

Her eyebrows rose and she sipped her tea.

"Go home, come here tomorrow with some fish and chips, and we'll talk when we both have had time to think."

I went to open my mouth, but she put a finger on my lips.

"I am not saying no; I am saying we need to think. I

have rushed headlong into a relationship once, and I do not want to make the same mistake twice."

I felt like saying that she had chased me, that I was being generous, that I had no ulterior motives, but I kissed her and went home.

At home I checked the progress in the basement. My two large searched had both ended with no further results, my new computer stack was ready and waiting, and my background search on Yaz had turned up another item. I idly checked it and then felt my stomach knot and my pulse rate rise as it was telling me that Yas visited Palestine when I thought she was on the smallholding. There were two downloads with the reference, one was of an Iranian passport for a Miss Maarah Klemp with a standard passport photo, and Maarah was Yaz's second name. The other was a full-face high-resolution photograph of her smiling at the camera. She was wearing a hijab, so I could not see her ears or hair, but the eyebrows were the same, the nose the same and the mouth smiling.

'How the hell were you there?' I asked myself.

I had a date and time and that she had crossed from Jordan, but I could not find her on any airline manifests. I turned back to the picture and studied it piece by piece on full magnification, but if it was a Photoshop, I couldn't find the seam. Finally, with my heart pounding,

I studied her mouth with the slight smile and the glint of a gold edged tooth. I stopped. Yaz did not have a gold edged tooth, in fact she did not have and cosmetic edging on any tooth, and I knew that because I already had her dental records. I could just see the two upper incisors and sighed, they fitted together perfectly and there was no gap, whereas Yaz had a noticeable space between them. I knew I had no choice and sent up a red flag using my new encrypted phone. Then, out of sheer curiosity, I manually accessed the database that had coughed up the information as I knew the exact location of the data. However, it did not give me a picture of Yaz, as now the data location was blank.

We met for breakfast on the Plaza.

"Tis an ill cook that cannot lick his own fingers," I murmured.

"Is love a tender thing? It is too rough, too rude, too boisterous, and it pricks like thorn," she replied.

She picked up her croissant.

"What is so damn urgent you spoil my Saturday?" She muttered, somewhat brusquely.

I swallowed.

"My background search on Yaz, it turned up a photo of her crossing into Palestine from Jorden when I know she was on the smallholding."

"Bloody hell, she is a plant!" Yvette replied.

I shook my head.

"It's good, very good, but I don't think it is a photoshop, I suspect a travelling clone?'

She looked blank.

"You choose a name of a non-passport holder and a look-alike photo, in this case probably using the Bulgarian ID card database, to create a false passport using your own photo for a one-off journey, or maybe a series of small journeys. Then you become someone else. Either that or the woman pretending to be Yaz is still in Palestine, but I doubt it."

Yvette groaned.

"So why call me now?"

I almost groaned.

"Because we have good links with the Mossad, and they need to know. I think I have found enough characteristics for her to be found again, but with their technology they may find more. And I was lucky as the data entry is no longer there, that takes a degree of infiltration they may not like."

Yvette fingered her croissant.

"You are sure it is not her?

I smiled and shook my head, but anyone can fill in a gap between teeth and add some gold paint, I just hoped upon hope that it she was just an innocent victim.

Decisions

I spent the rest of Saturday morning knocking off maintenance defaulters as a displacement activity, but by lunchtime, I knew I had a decision to make; did I believe Yaz or not? I set two more searches running, one for maintenance dodgers in deep cover and a second one for another possible set of minor terrorists and then took a walk to clear my head.

On my way back from the prom I walked up Southern Hill and past the viewing point. As I wandered past, I paused for a moment to look out to sea and then checked that the flat grey pebble lying next to the telescope had a black blemish near the centre. I casually kicked it over the edge and made my way into town, taking the North Boulevard to miss Yaz's shop, and ending up in the Town Hall Park with its picnic benches, model boating lake and play equipment and beyond to the bridal path that skirted the golf course and ended up at the little hamlet of Eastburgh Ferry. I did not go that far, instead halfway along, I sat down on a tree stump cut off at the right height to be a horse-mounting point. As I sat my left hand felt the crack in the side, and sure enough, there was a microSD card lurking in the crevice. I experienced some mixed emotions as this was a dead letter from Pete so I knew it would be urgent, while also knowing that he was circumventing normal lines of communication, so it was probably off the record. I carefully placed a piece of blank cardboard back in the crack and went home by a different route.

Once home, I plugged it, via an adapter, into my MacBook and ran the decryption routine. Pete did not go in for long messages and this was suitably terse. 'Major acting strangely. Has purple spotted you but will not say why and has not informed daughter. Simultaneously he has increased your pay, commensurate with your new security rating, and ringfenced your file. Daughter is trustworthy. Watch your back.'

I sat back. Purple spotting meant 'treat like royalty,' which indicated, 'keep away; keep an eye on and keep secure.' However, ringfencing my file, effectively making it 'eyes only,' was tantamount to letting me off the leash and allowing me to run free and unsupervised. I sat thinking for a while before adding our own database back in the requested deep and wide search and setting it running.

I drove out to see Yaz and passed her trailer park on my way to Jenny's Fish Bar, but sitting outside the park was a Border Force van with a short stocky chap studying the layout diagram, as well he might have because the numbering system was more than ad hoc. I suddenly got a bad feeling and drove in the second entrance and up to Yaz's to park on the standing beside the next trailer, which was an unlet rental. I dashed up to the door and she opened it wearing a onesie.

"No time to explain, the border force is after you; go and lie in the back of my cab," I said hurriedly.

She blinked.

"But I'm English, I have a UK…"

"Your passport is false, and they think you are Romanian."

Her mouth dropped open.

"It's me they are trying to intimidate," I said hastily. "You'll have to trust me."

I thrust my keys into her hands.

"You are entering Spooksville," I said in desperation.

She hesitated and then scampered to the truck and climbed in the back of the cab before there was the satisfying clunk of the door locks.

I dashed inside and hastily put away the cutlery and tomato ketchup she had got out on the small worktop, threw her topcoat and handbag into her bedroom, and closed the door. I opened a door to an empty bedroom and moved to the front door to study the scene. I then left the door open and went inside.

The border force chap turned up four minutes later

and stood outside the open door before he went to move inside. He was short, stocky and wearing a stab vest and eyed me with suspicion as I came out of the empty bedroom and looked at him.

"Border Force," he muttered. "Looking for a Maarah Kemp."

He held up the picture of the smiling woman in the hijab.

"Warrant card?" I said, looking into his cold brown eyes.

He ignored me.

"We have reason to believe that…" he continued.

I held up my ID card with my finger over my name.

"I really would like to see your warrant card," I said firmly.

He pulled out his card and showed it to me. I entered the number into my smartphone, and it told me that he was William Settle, known as Bill and he held a valid card. I sighed.

"Well Bill, we are both too late, our bird has flown," I said.

He was joined by a taller, younger, chap in a clean uniform.

"Not at home," said Bill to his colleague.

His colleague gave me a nasty smile, but at least he had his warrant card on display, so I knew he was Joe Brown.

"In that case, we'll just come in and take a look around," he said.

"Got a warrant?" I asked.

"Don't need one," he snarled. "If we have reason to believe…"

Bill laid a hand on his arm.

"He's Funny Farm, what he means is, he doesn't want our size ten boots trampling all over his investigation."

Joe grunted.

"What brought you here?" I asked.

Bill smiled, showing a set of truly dreadful teeth.

"Anonymous email tip-off. We got this photo plus passport details and an address."

I raised an eyebrow, and he tapped his nose.

"We have snouts in all sorts of places."

I managed a smile.

"So, you think she is…"

"Iranian," answered Joe.

I deliberately sighed.

"You are being used, check out the passport number, it is false, and she is not Iranian, Iraqi or Israeli."

"Nah, said Bill. "She's Roma, I'd recognise those features anywhere, it's all in the nose and the eye shape."

I pretended to look at the picture again.

"You could be right; we have not considered that."

He grinned somewhat smugly.

"Glad to be of help."

He turned to Joe.

"Come on, time to knock off."

They walked away over-casually, climbed in their van and drove off.

I stood watching the taillights.

"Stay put," I said into thin air. "They have not gone."

I went back inside to sit in the lounge and look out of the window from time to time and examine the contents of Yaz's handbag, which apart from an unused small aerosol of deodorant was innocuous. Suddenly I froze because I could see a tall figure flitting between caravans; Joe was not giving up quite so easily, rather he was following their protocol of 'never believe another occupant of a suspect's domicile.' I went back to the empty bedroom and flipped the mattress on its side and then the bed. I was rewarded with a small pouch of cheap cosmetics. Joe appeared at the door as I took out the lipstick and studied it carefully. I looked up.

"Back so soon?" I said sarcastically.

I waved the used lipstick about.

"Hopeful DNA, be a bit of confirmation."

"Terrorist?" he mused.

I shook my head.

"Scout," I replied.

He stuck his thumbs in his stab vest pockets, nodded, and swaggered off. I waited, but Bill picked him up and they drove off, hopefully for good.

Moves

As I watched the taillights a long-forgotten lecture on entrapment entered my mind. The lecturer had been an old hand and told us that sexual and financial entrapment were not the only tools of the trade as there was also emotional entrapment where you contravened the rules to help a friend, only the find out that the friend turned the tables and said they would report you unless… I doubted that this was such a case, but if I was being carefully set up was that the normally expected thought path? I took her handbag, closed the front door, and moved to my pickup to give a gentle tap on the window.

"It's me, and you are safe," I announced, to be rewarded with the door locks opening.

I climbed in the driver's seat, dropped the handbag into the back and started the engine, which I could do because the key transponder was within the cab area, and drove out of the site.

I parked up near Jenny's Fish Bar, climbed out of the front and climbed into the back. Yaz grabbed me like a limpet. I could feel her shaking, and now my adrenaline had stopped pumping, I was not in much better shape.

"What do you mean I am not British?" She stammered.

"Children have five-year passports, so there is no way your mother could have got you a ten-year passport when you were under sixteen," I explained. "And you are not registered on the passport database, but I know you have a Romanian birth certificate than says you were born in Oltenița."

She thumped me hard on the shoulder.

"You have been checking up on me; you bastard!"

I groaned because she could really pack a punch, and even a short stab was painful.

"I am sorry, but…"

She punched me again.

"Go on; say it was necessary!" She shouted.

I stayed silent and she took a deep breath.

"My father thought it better if I was Romanian like him, so he deliberately parked up over the border so I could be born there. A lot of Roma do not have their births registered, but he registered my birth and later insisted that we all had Bulgarian ID cards because he did not want bureaucratic hassle every time we were stopped by the police. Chantelle thought he was mad."

She suddenly grabbed me and hugged me tight.

"I am so sorry," I murmured. "I've got you into this, without me no one would care if you were British or Bavarian."

"They would if I tried to renew it, or get married or…" She paused. "How did I get into the country so easily if my passport is false?"

I laughed.

"Probably because you came in with a nun and they were not looking for illegals as they were fixated on your host's yacht"

After five minutes of deep hugging, we parted.

"Now what?" She asked.

"Now you have to trust me. I think I can regularise your status, but in the meantime, you cannot stay at your trailer. If the border force guys are doing their job properly, they will be back, probably in the early hours of Monday morning, maybe tomorrow."

She sniffed and blew her nose on a man-sized tissue.

"I heard the conversation; they think I am Iranian!"

I rubbed her arm.

"Spooks playing silly whatsits; they are getting at me, not you. Somewhere I am disturbing a hornet's nest and am being warned off."

She shivered.

"Tonight, I'll take you to mine, Monday you can see about an alternative if you don't want to stay at mine, but your trailer is now not safe."

She swallowed as if about to be sick.

"My work?"

"Safe as they have no connection, but make sure your rear door is unlocked."

She groaned.

"Then let's get it over with. The trailer is rented fully

furnished, so there are only my clothes, bedding, bicycle, and my short-wave radio."

My heart missed a beat.

"Short-wave radio?" I echoed.

She nodded.

"I used to listen to Radio Bulgaria, but they have now stopped transmitting, but there is still a 20-minute short-wave podcast from Germany."

There were no bin bags, but she had two duvet covers that we could fill, and we wrapped up the rest of her items in two fitted sheets and some pillowcases. Even so, it was nine-thirty before the pick-up was loaded and eleven-thirty before she was installed in the spare bedroom, but we had stopped for a miserable fish and chip meal at Jenny's on the way. We ended up in the kitchen drinking Horlicks. Biting my lip, I handed her a key.

"The alarm is simple, put your left index finger or middle finger in the reader and type in 1867, the year Karl Marx published Das Kapital, we'll put your fingerprints into the system before you go to bed."

She glanced up from the key.

"I hope your basement security door has a different code."

"It does," I replied.

I must admit that I felt washed out and she looked

somewhat drawn.

"I've sent a text to Caroline saying that I can't run the sound desk tomorrow and I think you are away. She can look after the desk for one week."

She sighed with relief and finished her drink.

"Fingerprints," I said.

She groaned, but I needed those fingerprints.

I woke up at 5 am to the sound of the toilet flushing and then relaxed. I was used to a silent house, but she had taken a seeming age to get to bed, and now had been to the toilet. I turned over, checked my alarm clock, and tried to sleep because I had an early morning appointment.

Entry into Spooksville

She did not have a dog with her, but she certainly had a scowl fit to curdle milk.

"Life is generally something that happens elsewhere.," she said as she pulled her black coat tighter around her.

"If you think squash is a competitive activity, try flower arranging," I replied.

"I am not your skivvy," she snapped. "I have a life!"

"Let's walk," I said.

We started walking along the 'clifftop.'

"Yesterday the border force tried to pick up Yaz using the photo of her supposedly going into Palestine, plus one of the forged Iranian passport. Somebody is mucking us about, and I hope it is not the Major."

She groaned.

"That bloody woman is nothing but trouble," she moaned.

"That woman is being used as a pawn, which is against our protocols unless they agree, and she has not agreed," I snapped back.

She stopped and shrugged her arms.

"And what am I supposed to do about it?"

I smiled.

"Under the Monserrat agreement, we can request a Residents Permit for her. I would prefer citizenship or a passport, but a Resident's Permit will do for now."

She stared at me as if I had grown two heads.

"I can't sanction that!" She exclaimed in horror.

I gave her a grim smile.

"No, but I believe I can."

She swallowed and licked her lips.

"You are not an operational manager, I cannot go waving your name about, questions might be asked."

I took a gamble.

"Use Fred Featherstone," I said with more confidence than I felt.

She blinked.

"Who is Fred Featherstone?"

I mentally crossed my fingers.

"It's a what, not a who. He is a virtual member of staff. His name is on the company's manifest, and he is certified up to high heaven, we use him as a cut-out, especially for jobs like this. The Home Office can look him up and as far as they are concerned, he is bona fide."

She rocked her head from side to side and rolled her eyes.

"Especially if you go down to London today to the Home Office emergency centre. It is what the centre is for, and if you have the right paperwork, they will not ask questions because they know it is best if they don't get an answer."

She raised her hands in horror.

"Oh no! Do this on a Sunday behind the Major's back,

he would have me boiled in oil."

I nodded.

"OK, I'll get MI5 to do it."

She closed her eyes as I was putting her between a rock and a hard place.

"And it's a trap," I said softly.

She opened her eyes.

"I'm listening," she said warily.

I moved closer and lowered my voice.

"If Yaz is clean, we have stopped her from getting caught up in our mess and she will just be grateful. If she is a plant, then down the line she could try to use the fact I got her a resident's permit via the back door as a lever. If she does, we have her cold."

Yvette clapped her hands.

"And I thought you were just an IT mole, you've been active."

I gave her a crooked smile. She huffed.

"Tomorrow, if I am successful, I'll leave you a letter in your PO box.."

She swung around and trounced off. I wondered just when I should tell her Yaz had moved in with me.

Back home Yaz was in the kitchen staring bleary-eyed into my fridge.

"Not yet stocked for two," I said over her shoulder.

She jumped and swung round.

"I did not hear you come in." her eyes narrowed. "I suppose you have been spooking."

"There are enough eggs and bread for boiled eggs and soldiers," I replied.

She rolled her eyes.

"I am not aged seven, I'll do scrambled egg on toast with those apologies that look like mushrooms and that tomato that is begging to be peeled."

I put my hands around her waist.

"You do not have to cook."

"No," she replied. "But I do have to clean that fridge out unless you want salmonella with your lunch."

It was a welcome breakfast, and by the third cup of coffee, she was a bit more compos mentis.

"Do you always start working this early?"

"Special conditions," I replied.

She laughed.

"You mean I've thrown a spanner in the works."

"And a lovely spanner it is too," I quipped.

She gazed out of the kitchen window.

"Will I be safe at work?"

I thought about it.

"It might be a risk on Monday, but by Tuesday I hope to have eliminated the risk," I said truthfully.

She stared at me, but I said no more. Eventually, she huffed.

"Is this what it's going to be like? Questions I can't ask and you full of secrets you can't tell?"

I reached over and held her hand.

"I have been upfront with you; I have not been secretive about the fact I work with databases looking for people who don't want to be found. I'll admit that there is some external baggage with that, but what I can tell you, I will." I held her hand tightly. "But I believe we can work it out, if we want to."

She did not pull had hand away and eventually nodded. "But if I am going to stay, I'd want that dog," she said softly. "When I woke up and you were out, I was scared. I didn't know if I'd have the courage to open the door if the bell rang, or even answer the phone, not after yesterday."

I smiled, telling Yvette that Yaz had moved in was one thing, telling operations I now had a guard dog, was something else entirely.

Settling

The young lady with lime green hair at the dog refuge laughed.

"The Koodle, oh that was snapped up, but count your blessings because it was a high-energy dog and somewhat independent and stubborn. What are you looking for?"

This was a question I had not thought about.

"A nonaggressive guard dog," replied Yaz.

I thought about saying that that was an oxymoron when the woman clapped her hands.

"We might have two you could look at, a six-year-old Labrador and a two-year-old Leonese."

"Leonese?" I echoed.

She half grinned.

"A cross between a Leonberger and a Bernese Mountain dog. He's a big lazy softie at heart, but both breeds are fiercely loyal to their family and can be particularly good with children." She hesitated. "But he might not win the prize for the most handsome dog on the block."

She set off to the kennels out the back, instantly causing a cacophony of barking and yelping, that she studiously ignored. She stopped by the Labrador, which glanced at us, put its head on one side, and walked away; clearly, we were not up to her specifications for owners. We moved on to the larger kennel at the end, the woman smiled, and I swear the dog smiled, but not at me, at

Yaz. It had a black head and back, and then a sort of mottled brown flank and legs, but none of the scruffy fur seemed to lie flat, and it was definitely large and beefy. Yaz reached through the bars of the cage, let it smell her hand and then patted its head; the large tail started a long slow sweep.

"You are a beauty," cooed Yaz.

Beauty was not a word I would have used. I looked at the nameplate.

"He's called Hesperus," I laughed.

"A noble name," said Yaz.

I tried for a little information.

"Why is he here?"

The young woman's face dropped.

"Owner was killed in a motorcycle accident, her mother said that her daughter doted on the dog, but she didn't have the room for such a generous-sized pooch." She went into sales mode. "Been with us two months as really large dogs are not popular, everyone wants the smaller breeds these days. Eats less than you would think, is fully trained, and does not need massive amounts of exercise, but could walk all day and all night if necessary. A bit like a St Bernard without the drool, it has a real personality all of his own."

She looked at Yaz.

"Fancy walking him?"

I spread the blanket on the rear seats and stepped back, almost without bidding Hesperus climbed up and lay down to let out a huge, contented sigh. I plugged his tether into the seatbelt stub and placed two large carrier bags plus a dog bed on the load bed before I tied them to the side. I had not expected the cost, it wasn't the dog as that was just a £50 donation, it was the pet insurance, the harness, the dog bowls, the dog bed, and a stout lead plus a starter pack of dog food. However, it was an investment, an investment in Yaz's happiness and our personal security.

Back at base I removed the door for the understairs cupboard and put his dog bed inside, he stood outside surveying it.

"In you go," said Yaz, making a shooing motion.

He turned around, backed in and lay half on the dog bed and half off. After a moment he came out. Yaz moved his dog bed to where he had been lying and once again, he backed in and laid down, this time to give a contented sigh. I smiled, he certainly had a personality, but he was also lying so he could see the front door and in his own way put himself on guard.

While Yaz insisted on cleaning the fridge and freezer, I went down to the basement and checked my searches, there were absolutely no results, although my deep and wide search now indicated that it would take eight months, which was good as it has started off estimating two years, so the estimated run time, as normal, was coming down. I did a rough calculation and guessed that it should come down to two and a half weeks, considering what it was looking for and where it was searching, that was amazing.

Mid-afternoon I went to the Post Office. There was a pasty-faced woman behind the counter I had never seen before, but she was wearing her ID badge, that said she was Linette Dawn.

"Post Office Box 117," I murmured.

She tapped her computer screen.

"You have a password," she said in an exquisite Buckinghamshire accent.

"Zadok the Priest," I replied.

She nodded.

"ID?" She inquired.

I showed her my driving licence, or rather the driving licence I keep for such occasions, and she nodded to go and rummage on the shelves. I expected a brown envelope, but she came back with a parcel the size of a hardback novel.

Back in my basement I put my 'driving licence' away and opened the parcel. Inside was a second box with a note on top. 'Monserrat Agreement modified when we were not looking, now only applies to protection staff and defectors sponsored by MI6, but fortunately, the wording is ambiguous. Residence permits are not now included. Had to talk to my supervisor – not The Major – and this was all we could do in the time frame. He insisted on the extra items to make it look bona fide if questions are asked."

I dropped the note into my shredder and opened the box, inside was a passport; an ID card, a diminutive Smith & Wesson 317 .22 snub nose revolver; and a new smartphone that I would not trust in a million years. I put the smartphone in a tin box and went upstairs.

She had just put the kettle on, so I waited until we were sitting down.

"I have good news and bad news," I said softly, sliding her new passport across the desk.

Her eyebrows rose and she picked it up with a look of wonderment on her face.

"You can do that, get a passport at a click of your finger?"

"Spooksville," I said smugly. "We live in a parallel universe, but there are strings."

Her eyes narrowed.

"Look at the back page of the passport," I prompted.

She opened the passport and spluttered.

"I'm down as Mrs Yaz Unity Parks!'

I nodded.

"It needed to be clear of your real name, but viable."

Her eyes narrowed.

"I hope you don't think that just because…"

I raised a hand.

"You and I are on a road to unity, I hope; this is just an identity that will keep you safe."

She glanced at what else I was trying to hide.

"There's more, I can sense that there is more."

I swallowed and went into quiet talking mode.

"Even I cannot conjure up a passport from thin air as we have to have a justification that satisfies the Home Office."

I slid over the ID card. She stared at it.

"MI7 Protection Officer! What the hell does that mean?"

I managed a smile.

"It means you either look after a safe house or act as a bodyguard for MI7."

I did not add that to my knowledge, we did not have any safe houses, nor use any of our own close protection officers. There is also no such unit as MI7 as we are really a virtual part of the Joint Intelligence Organisation, but she did not need to know that. I slid over the gun.

"And you are normally armed."

She looked at the gun as if it were an alien entity that had materialised in front of her out of thin air.

"It's a Smith & Wesson 317 .22 eight-round snub nose revolver. You'd probably have trouble hitting a barn door at twenty yards, but they make a very loud bang and have a spectacular muzzle flash," I said softly.

I did not tell her that it was loaded with low-velocity soft-nosed bullets to reduce the recoil, but also ensure that if ever she did shoot someone it would leave a decent-sized hole.

She looked into my eyes.

"You said what you did was not dangerous, just sneaky."

"I did not lie," I said. "But it is the price I am being made to pay for your passport."

She bit her bottom lip.

"You did not order this?"

I truthfully shook my head but reached out and held her hand.

"But you now have a passport that will withstand the utmost scrutiny."

She squeezed my hand and I smiled. However, I did not tell her that I now had another problem as her passport had a wonderful photograph of her that I did not know existed, so just where did Yvette get it from?

Rubbing Along

We paused on our walk around a wooded area called The Grove as Hesperus, who Yaz had rechristened as Hesp, stopped to sniff a bush and lift his leg to leave his mark. We resumed walking.

"I have told the boss I will be in tomorrow; he was quite glad as he'd had to man the shop himself all day." She murmured.

Suddenly Hesp stopped dead as a yapping terrier shot out from under a bush. For a good five seconds, he did nothing as the terrier danced and yapped in front of him, and then he let out a low rumbling growl. The terrier stopped barking, backed away and then ran off.

"Passive-aggressive, you are a good boy," announced Yaz as she rubbed his head.

We turned for home and walked back along the footpath we had originally used.

"Used to have a dog when I was ten, she was called Snatch and was a mixture of two mongrels. She was not very big, and I went everywhere with her, but she grew ill and I think Father shot her, but he would never say."

"I promise I will never shoot Hesp," I said dutifully.

Hesp stopped to sniff a wayside flower. He sniffed it twice and then gently bit it off its stalk to chew it slowly; I decided that I had better watch my roses.

Tuesday, after Yaz had gone to work I went into the

basement. I was examining my new computer triad when Hesp tentatively came down the steep steps and stood at the bottom. He sniffed the air and looked at a bare corner. I still had some of the cardboard from the fridge/freezer box, so I laid it in the corner four sheets thick. He wandered over and lay down, fidgeted and sat up. I got the message and went upstairs to fetch an old sleeping bag. I laid this on top of the cardboard and he lay down on it, sighed, and closed his eyes. However, he was laying facing the steps, it seemed to be a trait of his.

When Yaz arrived home, I had a nut roast and salad ready, she kissed me on the cheek, visited the bathroom, and in no time at all we were sitting and eating.

"Good day?" I ventured.

"Average," she replied.

"Tired?" I asked.

"Middling," she responded before touching my arm.

"Please no small talk, let's just eat."

We ate for a few moments.

"But it highlights a problem," she sighed.

"Problem?"

She nodded as she added a little more pickle.

"What do I ask? Are your computers ticking away nicely? Have you had a good spook today?"

I understood.

"You can ask, and if I've had a good day finding

maintenance dodgers or the odd bigamist, I will tell you, otherwise…"

She grimaced and I changed tack.

"I don't want to keep secrets from you, but I am not allowed to tell you, partially for your own protection, and partially because if you did know, who could you tell?"

"Spooks anonymous," she quipped.

She sat back.

"You will not talk to me about colleagues, you cannot tell me what you are doing, and you live in a world of secret handshakes, and you want me to be content with that."

I could see where she was coming from and had no answers to give.

"On the other hand," she said softly. "I know you will not grow cannabis in the basement, you will not expect me to dig over a plot by lantern light or pump you up a bath when I am dead on my feet."

I reached out to touch her arm.

"We can work it out," I paused. "What brought this on?"

She sighed.

"Benny, my boss, he spent twenty minutes telling me about his wife starting up a self-help mother and toddler group, and I realised that I can never talk about you in that way."

"You can tell him how fanatical I am about preserving a retro sound system, or that what I do is highly technical and boring IT." I quipped.

She smiled, put her fork down and offered Hesp some nut roast. He sniffed and backed away.

"I didn't think dogs were supposed to eat nuts," I said.

"Please don't tell me I have to eat it," she said to Hesp. I put my fork down.

"OK, it's dreadful," I sighed.

"At least you tried," she replied. "Hugh never tried, except once when he thought he'd do a stir fry, but we didn't have any olive oil and he tried to use vegetable margarine instead. In the end, we had to put the wok out of its misery and bury it where we thought the iron would be good for the soil."

She examined the nut roast.

"I'd frozen it, but I didn't realise until I'd unwrapped it that it said, 'Not for Freezing' on the bottom," I confessed.

She suddenly smiled.

"Blame me, I've cleared out your freezer of everything I thought was frozen into oblivion, but left this as you'd clearly dated it two months ago."

"Fourteen months," I said drolly. "I didn't add the year."

At 2:30 am I got up to answer a call of nature and

padded downstairs. I didn't bother to turn the lights on as there was plenty of moonlight. I went to the toilet and when I came out Hesp was standing by the front door. I judged that he probably needed a pee as well and led him through the lounge and into the kitchen area, it was here I opened the back door and turned on the conservatory lights to see a startled young man kneeling in front of the conservatory. He looked at me, he looked at Hesp and took off like a scalded rabbit running down the slight slope to my rear fence as if the hounds of hell were after him. By the time I had the patio door slid open he was halfway down the garden. Hesp, despite his size, took off like a rocket, only giving one bark to tell his prey he was in pursuit. The guy veered toward one corner of my garden, used the garden bench at the end as a launch pad and dived over my four-foot rear fence that was covered in climbing roses. As he moved upwards Hesp took a snap and locked onto the heel of the chap's left trainer; he had sufficient momentum to make it over the fence but left his trainer behind. There was a thud and a scream as he landed. I wondered if he had managed to clear the ditch on the other side of the fence. I thought for a moment, as Hesp circled, that he was going to jump the fence and go after him, but doggy sense took over and he decided that he was not going to leap into the dark. I grabbed the emergency torch off its battery charger and trotted down the garden to stand on the bench and look over the fence into the field beyond. About twenty yards into the field the guy was sitting down, his left shoulder looked somewhat displaced, and he already had his smartphone out and was using it with one hand. I waited and a couple of minutes later an electric motorbike bumped across the field, and he climbed on with some obvious discomfort in his left ankle. I climbed off the bench and Hesp brought me his prize, a nice white size 11 trainer and dropped it at my feet.

"Good boy," I said rubbing his head. "Good boy."

I got a sense that he had rather enjoyed his escapade and he sprayed the corner of the garden and checked out the fence as if on patrol. Not only did I have the trainer, but I also had a thin white sock, and lying between them an ID card. I studied it with my torch.

"Vincent Martin of Padlock Securities," I said to myself. Just then the lounge light came on and Yaz appeared in the doorway wearing a thin dressing gown.

"Did I hear a scream?" She said in alarm.

I smiled at Hesp.

"We have it under control," I said rather smugly.

The Range

Yaz surveyed the low concrete building and sighed.

"You do bring me to the nicest of places."

"If you have a gun, it is best to learn how to use it properly," I said practically.

We climbed out and ambled towards the front door. I rang the bell, showed my ID card to the CCTV camera, and we were let into a lobby where an army corporal inspected our ID cards and checked them out on his computer.

"Never heard of MI7," he muttered.

"That is the point," I replied.

His eyebrows rose as he surveyed his screen.

"Joint Intelligence Organisation," he said softly.

He pressed his green button and let us through.

"This is military," Yaz said quietly.

"If you want to use a gun, go to the experts," I quipped.

She was not impressed.

The gun tutor on duty was a female sergeant with greying blonde hair in a pigtail, a weather-beaten face and J Merriweather embroidered on her breast pocket. She eyed Yaz's .22 revolver with suspicion.

"My colleague has just been issued this," I murmured. "She needs to practice with it and then learn to use a Mossberg

She looked at Yaz.

"Ever fired a gun before?"

Yaz shook her head. She handed her some ear defenders, a pair of safety glasses, and wound the target back to ten metres. She took Yaz through the correct stance and then put two bullets in the bullseye. She handed the gun to Yaz, who fired one bullet and just nicked the edge of the target.

"Don't close one eye," the sergeant yelled. "And try for a smoother pull."

Yaz shot again and hit the inner ring. I decided it was time to withdraw.

I spent fifteen minutes practising with my 9mm Hellcat pistol and then left it with a corporal for a check over and service. I moved to the outside range and found Yvette using a Heckler & Koch with a telescoping sight and hitting a target 150 metres away. I waited until she finished and took off her ear defenders.

"I am glad you are on my side," I said dryly.

"Major's insistence," she muttered. "I hope I never have to use one in anger."

I handed her the Padlock Securities ID card.

"Found one of their guys last night, trying to attach a vibrator microphone to my conservatory window. He wears size 11 trainers and is probably walking with a limp. I took your advice and got a dog."

She nodded.

"You took Hesperus, the kennel maids there said it was a nice young couple, but he walked with a rolling gait and figured it was you. Nice choice, no burglar in his right mind would tackle him. I've walked him a couple of times and he is easy to manage but rather likes eating flowers, I am told that he is partial to Nasturtium."

She looked at the ID card.

"Want them checked out?"

"Want them frightened off, and I would love to know just who employed them, and who told them where I lived. I'd also like the Zambo's tomorrow morning after Yaz has left for work. Vibrator microphones are one thing, reflected lasers are quite another," I said quietly.

She nodded.

"And thanks for the passport," I added.

She rolled her eyes.

"It's all about a comma."

I raised an eyebrow.

"The modified Monserrat agreement says that it now only applies to protection staff, and defectors sponsored by MI6. Because there is a comma after protection staff it can be said that the caveat MI6 only applies to defectors; at least that's how my boss read it. However, it is passports only and you know the rest as we had to prove they were the staff."

"Thank you anyway," I replied.

She turned the ID card over in her hand.

"You are stirring up a hornet's nest."

"Not me, it's the search asked for by those two you introduced." I hesitated, but I needed her on my side. "They are mole hunting and I suspect the mole wishes to bury my search and live in peace."

She nodded.

"You're saying trust no one."

I shrugged.

"We all have to trust someone, and I have been told I can trust you."

Her eyebrows rose, but she didn't comment.

Yaz climbed back into the cab.

"Why was I taught how to use and clean that nasty short shotgun with the peculiar hand stock? Jennifer clearly thought it was the perfect weapon for short-range mayhem."

"Revolver training, OK?" I casually asked.

She thumped me.

"You are changing the subject, but I need to know."

I nodded.

"There is one behind the hot water tank and a box of shells tucked under the tank. It is standard issue."

Her mouth dropped open.

"Jennifer talked about defending staircases and shooting through walls if necessary. She even got me to blast away at a breeze block, just to show me how effective it was."

She suddenly smiled.

"She also got me to fire my little revolver without wearing ear defenders, just so I got used to how loud it was and told me that it was a short-range defence weapon."

She put her seat belt on.

"Have you got a gun?"

I went to answer, and she held up a hand.

"I don't want to know."

"I don't carry," I said. "It is stashed in my basement; again, it is standard issue."

She shivered.

"Jennifer was nice, but I never want to come here again."

I nodded, next time it would be the police firing range.

I started to drive out.

"Who was the woman you were talking to? I went to the loo, and I could see you on one of the screens in some sort of operations room."

I hesitated and she groaned.

"Don't tell me, Spooksville."

I smiled.

"I thought we might like to go out to Dunwich Heath, I suspect Hesp might like it there," I said carefully.

Cleanliness next to Godliness

The Zambos turned up just after nine and started sweeping for bugs and other electronic nasties. There were three, one took the house, excluding the basement, one took the garden, and one surveyed the local area. They made regular three-monthly visits in the guise of a cleaning firm, which in a way they were. By mid-afternoon, they had finished and found nothing until their wandering cleaner returned looking smug.

"Nothing," he said. "Except that there's a derelict end terrace house two streets over and their satellite dish appeared to have swivelled in its mountings, but it was pointing directly at here. The place is derelict, so I exercised a duty of care and removed it before it fell on someone's head but believe me it was firmly mounted, and the coax cable was nowhere near as old as the dish."

"Wi-Fi hunting," said one of the others.

They packed up their gear and one of them paused.

"That old Russian short-wave radio your guest has got, when it's in band 2 it emits a 201Mhz signal, some car trackers use frequencies like that."

I swallowed.

"Intentional?"

He shrugged.

"Who knows? It's so battered and badly bodged up it is probably just coincidental. There's nothing odd about it, except that it's badly made. Personally, I'd buy a new

148

one."

They left and I went back to my basement and let Hesp out. He went into every room sniffing and looking at me as if I had let in something nasty.

I had one last check on progress before I started dinner and found that my deep search had already turned up a result. I checked it out and my blood ran cold because it had thrown up the last person I had expected; me. Further interrogation indicated that I fulfilled the criteria because I had seen a Løytnant Haugen of the Norwegian Army six times in the last three years. That was true, but we had been working closely on improving our mutual data searches and every meeting was in my logbook and sanctioned by The Major. However, I resolved to carefully assess any further results lest I throw some poor unsuspecting clerk to the dogs for no reason at all.

When Yaz came home she looked deadbeat and after eating my dubious offering of lamb stew we went into the conservatory, and she put her feet up.
"Bad day?"
"Deliveries and a couple of large orders to prepare, and Benny had to go to the hospital because his four-year-old decided to stuff a Lego brick up her nose."
I nodded.

"I'm told I had to go to A&E when I was five because I drank nearly half a bottle of cherry brandy. I'm told, I slept for two days."

She smiled and closed her eyes; she was asleep in less than a minute.

The following morning there were no results on the deep search, but my hunt for maintenance dodgers had thrown up three names. One was deceased, one was alive and sculling about in Durham and the third was happily married for a third time (when he had not quite divorced his second wife.) I gave the results to the appropriate family courts and took a Hesp for a walk, ending up at the viewing point. Yvette had the Staffie again and I expected fireworks, but the two dogs sniffed each other, at both ends and settled down between us.

"No man or woman born, coward or brave, can shun his destiny," she murmured.

I hesitated because Homer's Iliad was not high on my quotes list, but she was right because it was after noon on the third Thursday of the month, so it could be Homer or Socrates.

"Beauty! Terrible Beauty! A deathless Goddess-- so she strikes our eyes!" I eventually replied.

She nodded.

"You've chosen your dog?" I ventured.

She nodded.

"Enyo has found a place in my heart."

I laughed.

"The Roman goddess who loved bloodshed."

She raised an eyebrow.

"Really, I thought it was just a cute name."

She gazed out to sea.

"Padlock Securities doesn't exist and the phone number on the card is just an unregistered mobile, not that I expected anything else, but I found your man with a limp. He visited Bury St Edmunds A&E, had a dislocated shoulder reset and an ankle strapped up and gave his name as Gerald Greenway. The same chap, easily identified because he had an NHS crutch and a scratch on his cheek, flew from Stansted to Bucharest on the early morning flight using a Moroccan passport in the name of Taleb Tazi, which is interesting as he has blue eyes. We think he flew out of Craiova to Portugal later in the day, but we have not alerted the appropriate authorities as he was just in transit, and we think he took the first available flight just to leave the country."

"Any ideas who employed him?"

She shook her head.

"But we have the registration number of that electric motorbike from the CCTV at Bury Hospital, it comes back to a tractor in Huddersfield. However, we have asked the police to add it to their ANPR system."

We were disturbed by my phone pinging, so I glanced

and read the text. I groaned.

"That's Yaz, she's holed up in the loo of the shop where she works because the Border Force is back trying to pick her up. I'll go, you do what you can from here."

She raised her hands in despair.

"Be inventive," I said as I left at a brisk trot.

When I arrived, Bill was standing guard at the front of the shop, standing with his arms folded, and Joe was out the back thumping on the loo door. Bill retreated towards the back of the shop as I arrived, eyeing the dog warily.

"You can stop that, I yelled at Joe. She is not the person you are looking for."

He smirked.

"She is according to the lady in the site office, she told us she worked here. I don't care who you are or what ID you have, she is coming with us."

I smelt belligerence in the air.

"I have her passport number," I said in exasperation.

"And we are supposed to trust you?" he sneered. "Not again, not this side of the Zambesi."

He took a step towards me, which was a mistake as Hesp gave out a low throaty growl.

"And you can call your dog off, because under…"

He stopped because his phone rang. He looked at the screen and answered the call. A mystical look came over his face. He handed Bill the phone.

"It's the boss, for you."

"Tell Charlie I'll ring him later," Bill replied.

Joe shook his head.

"Not Charlie; Melinda."

Bill did not quite stand to attention, but it was close.

"William Settle here ma'am," he purred into his phone.

He listened, glanced at me, and ground his teeth.

"Fully understood ma'am," he half-croaked before he closed the call.

He took a deep breath and spoke to his colleague.

"She's funny farm and we are not, under any circumstances to harass her or seek her extradition."

Joe rolled his eyes upwards.

"I think we should check her out down the…"

"We have been ordered off," snapped Bill somewhat harshly. "I was told it was for reasons above my pay grade and I am not going to argue with a Senior Director, and neither are you if you have any sense."

He glared at me.

"You're doing?"

I shrugged.

"Someone is playing games to unsettle us and using you as pawns. And believe me, the lady here has a bona fide UK passport."

"I don't doubt it," snarled Joe. "But is it her that is bona fide or just her paperwork?"

The loo door opened and Hesp barged his way passed them to sit at her side as Yaz emerged, white-faced and angry. Bill turned to her.

"My apologies madam, apparently we have been misled."

"I told you I had a British Passport, but would you listen? I sincerely hope that you treat other people with a little more respect!" She shrilled at them.

Joe went to answer, but Bill grabbed him by the arm and dragged him out of the shop. Yaz rushed forward into my arms, and Hesp went to the shop entrance, just to make sure they were leaving.

Worrying Trends

By lunchtime on Friday, I had a problem, my deep and wide search had turned up 32 results. Normally you set the criteria so tight you only got one or two results, so 32 was approaching the absurd. However, I let it run, mainly because experience told me that as the search progressed some of these 'results' would disappear. Just then my police-instigated search turned up a name and I immediately phoned it through because this was a different type of search, it was hunting for a particular person, but a person about whom I had lots of search criteria, whereas my 'deep' search was fishing to see what it could find.

Almost as I was due to leave because I had said I would pick Yaz up from the shop, her search turned up something else. If it was to be believed, she had been in Moldova and crossed over into Romania at the Joint Contact Center Galati, which was worrying as in that part of the world it would be easy to go from Russia to Moldova and then into Romania. However, the date was when she was working on her smallholding with Hugh, which would be just right to muddy the waters; there was no accompanying documentation, and her passport was supposedly Andorran. I did a quick check and, as I half expected, there was an Andorran passport with that number, but the recipient had a wide mouth and shorter eyebrows. It was more games, and it was beginning to worry me.

By the time I arrived, she had almost finished and was collecting some fruit and veg for our use. I gave her a hug and a kiss.

"No problems today?"

She shook her head.

"But I saw that Bill and Joe, they went into the Chinese restaurant and dragged out a cook, I can't believe they have the right to do that. Joe even gave me a wave, but it had 'I'll get you one day,' written all over it."

She looked at a large box of mixed fruit and veg.

"Don't suppose we could go home via Hudson's Farm over at Heritage Farm out near this side of Captain's wood? This lot is for them, but the wife rang as her car won't start and they run a B&B?"

I smiled.

"Of course, Hesp will enjoy the ride and we might find a place to walk him and help us all unwind."

Hudson's Farm turned out to be in the middle of nowhere, but I guess the solitude was part of the attraction, that and the walks down to the River Alde. We stopped by a wood on the way back and Hesp wandered about sniffing and spraying every fifth tree while we walked hand in hand. Eventually, we started for home. The lanes were narrow and winding until we popped out onto a straight stretch, it was then I noticed the black Mitsubishi pickup on our tail. As soon as we hit the straight, it flashed its lights and started to pull alongside.

"Someone in a hurry," I remarked.

Yaz moved her head to look in the wing mirror and then turned in her seat to look out.

"The passenger window is down, and he has a gun!" She exclaimed.

I instinctively flipped the car into 'sports' mode and thumped my foot to the floor. The automatic gearbox took a couple of long seconds to think before we felt it accelerate. However, it was a no contest as the Mitsubishi had a larger engine and, even though it was undoubtedly heavier, it only dropped back a few yards before it started to gain. However, I had gained time and we were now running out of straight road. I glanced at the sat-nav, which was still running, and realised that there was a sharp corner coming up, one where it looked innocent, but in no time at all went through almost 120°. I waited until their bonnet was level with the door.

"Brakes!" I yelled before I stamped on the brake pedal. The car did its job, I was doing an emergency stop and it pushed the brakes on harder. I heard Yaz grunt as her seatbelt locked and Hesp yelped as he was catapulted forward and stopped by his harness. The Mitsubishi shot passed and I could see the wheels almost locking as it turned into the bend we saw the load-bed rise and then spin away. We stopped just before the bend.

"You have done an emergency stop," intoned a voice from beside the roof lights. "Do you wish…"

I cancelled the automated police call and took off my seatbelt.

"You got your gun?" I gasped.

She nodded picked her handbag up from beside her and handed it to me.

"Stay here," I said. "Look after the dog, if you hear firing, call the police."

I got out and raced along the nearside hedge to peer around. The pickup was stuck firmly into a large tree that had been waiting for years for someone to miss the turn. There was steam rising from the crushed bonnet and debris thrown along the hedgerow. I pulled open the passenger door that creaked somewhat, but opened, a testimony to modern car safety. Inside there was talc in the air and the smell of burning from the exploding airbags, plus a loud ticking from the damaged engine as it tried to cool down without any coolant. There were two men wearing charcoal grey suits, tough-looking black shoes, and black leather gloves, all they needed were some black shades and they would be CIA stereotypes, but I doubted that these pair were CIA because I was still alive. The driver was slumped against the side window and groaning, but the passenger was moving and trying to cut through his seatbelt with a wicked-looking flick-knife. I stuck Yaz's gun in his ear and removed the knife. On the floor were a flare gun and a Remington TAC 14 short-barrelled, short-stock shotgun, which told me these guys were serious. I pulled back his jacket and relieved him of a Colt Trophy 9mm pistol, which is far too large to be a concealed carry weapon for normal mortals, except the passenger was a large man with thick neck muscles and bulging biceps. I also took his wallet.

"Your colleague, is he carrying?" I growled.

There was a slight shake of the head.

"I don't believe you," I snarled.

"I want his gun and his wallet, or you get a messed-up brain."

He tentatively reached over and passed me a Glock 42 and another wallet.

"Who are you."

"Padlock Securities," He answered, but his accent was South African.

I was running out of time because their automated call system had made contact and was stating that there had been an accident and giving the location. I picked up the shotgun.

"Who are you working for?" I asked harshly.

"Anonymous email and money in a left luggage locker," moaned the driver.

I had expected nothing less.

"And your orders?

"Warn you off," said the passenger. "That's all, just a flare at your windscreen."

"So, you came tooled up like a chef at a barbeque," I replied.

I looked down the road, but I could only see the bonnet of my truck.

"Word to the wise, you should have used the shotgun on my rear hub, learn from your mistakes."

I stood back and the chap went to grab me, but he was still locked in his seatbelt.

"Stay where you are until I have gone," I growled. "For your personal safety."

He nodded.

"I'm leaving you the flare gun," I murmured. "I'd guess you have ten minutes to sort yourselves out. I know who you are, so go home."

I took some pictures with my phone before I trotted back to my truck.

Yaz was in the rear, so I dropped my booty onto the floor of the car.

"Hesp OK?"

"Seems to be," she replied. "But I'm staying in the back

with him, I don't want him frightened."

I managed to drive past the wreck by just squeezing through the gap with my mirrors folded.

"You just leaving them there!" Yaz yelled in horror.

"Both alive and fairly battered, but we do not want to be around when the police arrive. They have been called out by their car's automated system." I replied.

I went about a half mile down the road, turned into a by-road and parked at a farm entrance. I then stood up on the load bed. After a couple of minutes, smoke started billowing into the air and I could just hear the howl of a police siren. Protocol demanded that I leave. I climbed back inside and took a deep breath before I used the car's connection to my smartphone to make a call.

"Raining's Hardware," said a chirpy voice.

"Yankee doodle dandy, repeat yankee doodle dandy. Allan Parks Zulu, Alpha, Romeo, one, nine, six, zero. Need an immediate rendezvous, am near Iken in Suffolk."

I waited.

"Can you make RAF Woodbridge, repeat, RAF Woodbridge; do you need a doctor?"

I smiled.

"No, but would value a vet."

"Yankee doodle dandy," said the voice and rang off.

Rendezvous

The guards at the gate let us in but escorted us to a building not too far inside labelled RAF Police. Two burly corporals took us inside to the officer's quarters, checked our IDs, and settled us down, giving Hesp a bowl of water and us two mugs of tea and a tin of shortbread biscuits. I held Yaz's hand and could feel her trembling, but it was a mutual tremble.

"Were they trying to kill us?" She asked, somewhat tremulously.

I sought for a diplomatic answer.

"Warn us off, it was a flare gun, probably wanted to get ahead and fire it at the windscreen, it can be somewhat intimidating."

I tried for a smile, but it was just as likely they would have tried to fire it into the cab if their intention had been more than a 'harmless' warn-off.

"That was a shotgun and a bloody great pistol you put on the car floor," she half shrilled.

"Pistol from the driver's shoulder holster and shotgun from the car's floor, I do not believe that they intended to use them." I hesitated. "I do not think that they are professionals, the revolver is too bulky, and a professional would have used the shotgun on a rear wheel hub, that would have sent the required message without endangering them." I licked my lips. "And the driver had not had any advanced driving training, if so,

162

he would have barged us when we accelerated."

"Oh whoopie," she said sarcastically. "We were only attacked by amateurs."

I smiled, but I had peeped in one of the wallets; there was an ID for Padlock Securities, but the driving licence was French.

Yaz frowned.

"I still can't believe you just left them there."

I squeezed her hand.

"Risk assessment; if I wasn't prepared to shoot them, I probably couldn't contain them as they are muscular and might not have the same scruples as me, and I certainly wasn't going to involve you."

She groaned.

"We have Hesp, they wouldn't argue with Hesp."

I swallowed.

"If they had another gun, they would have shot him. People like that…"

Thankfully the door opened, and a civilian brought us two plates of steaming curry and some fruit, so I didn't have to explain any more, but I knew the company representative may not be so understanding.

Fortunately, it was Pete. He wandered in carrying the type of large briefcase favoured by airline pilots. He sat down and gently debriefed us and studied the wallets and guns I had retrieved. "The police have detained them, but they claim to have lost their wallets and passports in the blazing wreck. However, their prints are on the South African criminal database, they are basically a pair of rent-a-thugs, but they flew in on Zambian passports and knew which car you drive, so someone put them in place. They are firmly in the 'no comment' school of interviewing techniques. The police are currently holding them on passport violations as illegal immigrants. We have requested that they be held for 24 hours and released on bail pending deportation to Zambia."

"What!" exclaimed Yaz. "Just let them go!"

Pete nodded.

"The police do not know they had guns, and we want to see who they contact. We have quietly searched their hotel room and found an unregistered phone, which we are now monitoring. They may have other ways of contacting the people who hired them, but we have most bases covered."

I smiled, but there were a million ways of sending or dropping a message specially designed to evade detection. He turned to me.

"Best you change your vehicle, we do not want a repeat."

What he meant was that if I had a different car and there was a repeat it either meant I was being monitored or there was an internal leak. I shook my head.

"It is not a company car. If you remember the deal I struck with our lords and masters was that to stay on the books and have my fitness level ignored, I had to buy my own house, my transport and set up my own computing facilities."

He looked like he had swallowed a lemon.

"I did not know that; it may have to be revisited," he said softly.

"It was termed 'arm's length data capabilities."

He let out a barking laugh.

"Arm's length? You have got to be…"

He smiled at Yaz.

"Have you seen a vet?"

"RAF chief dog handler, he gave our dog the OK, but said it was lucky he was wearing a harness, because had it just been a dog collar, he would have broken his neck."

He stood up.

"My daughter will doubtless be in touch. You are free to go home, but please try not to annoy the natives."

It was a frosty drive home because Yaz hardly spoke, so when we stopped, I said what was on my mind.

"I didn't sign up for this, not chasing off eavesdroppers in my garden or driving thugs into trees. If it doesn't stop, I shall resign and go into commercial data mining. There is plenty of work out there, it is just a little bit more difficult to sort the good from the bad. By that, I mean data mining to improve people's lives, not better target adverts or steal a march on competitors."

"Finding maintenance defaulters sounds good to me," she murmured.

I sighed.

"It is, but it doesn't make enough profit to feed a flea, let alone run a family."

She reached out and held my hand.

"You're doing this for me, I can tell."

I took a deep breath.

"You didn't sign up for this, if I am to keep you then…"

She squeezed my hand.

"Let's hope it will pass. You are right, we could not bring up a child like this; we could if you were just doing the odd bit of spooking and she could legitimately say 'Daddy hunt's down people who leave their children,' but not if she had to say she that had no idea what daddy did, but it was very dangerous."

"She?" I echoed.

Yaz smiled.

"I am hoping for a she, but a he would do."

She let go and climbed out to take Hesp off for a sniff and spray. I analysed what I had said and was surprised to discover that I had meant every word.

At just past midnight my bedroom door opened and

Yaz crossed the room to slip in beside me. She felt cold and smelt of shampoo and shower. I instinctively held her close.

"I'm frightened Allan," she whispered. "I've found you and I don't want to lose you, but I am not sure I can spend my life looking over my shoulder and worrying about you every time you left the house."

I held her tight.

"I don't want to lose you either," I murmured. "You are finding a loving corner in my heart I didn't know I had." We kissed, and I instinctively knew that I was running into sexual danger, but I didn't care, I just didn't care.

Rendevous2

Once Yaz had gone to work for Saturday duty I went into the basement. The maintenance defaulter search had turned up a potential in Wigan, Yaz's search had not found anything, and the deep search had turned up 81 results. It confirmed my worst fears; I had to go back to school.

As far as I could see, the fens around Little Thetford looked the same, and the large farmhouse was still painted in an odd shade of beige, beige with a hint of pink, or as the instructors used to say, beige with a tinge of the blood we would sweat. I parked up and was met by a young blonde woman in dungarees who looked fit enough to throw me over the small barn. I showed her my ID card.

"Just popped in for a yarn with the chief," I murmured. I got the ghost of a smile.

"Appointment?"

"Just passing the time of day."

Her eyes narrowed.

"We make a living by what we get, but we make a life by what we give," she murmured.

"The farther backward you can look, the farther forward you can see," I replied.

She nodded.

"Mind if I pat you down?" She asked, indicating that she

would not take no for an answer.

I let her pat me down and she stood back.

"You know where she is," she said.

I pulled the flick knife out of where I had hidden it in the collar at the back of my neck. Her eyes widened.

"You should have gone through the quote routine as soon as you saw my card, and your pat down was good, but you did not pat me between the shoulder blades and missed this plus flare gun I have loaded with a shotgun cartridge and stuffed up the back of my bra," I jested.

She groaned, but it was a matter of honour that tutors always got items through the pat down when students were on guard duty.

The Chief's rooms were still on the rear of the first floor, and I knocked and entered. Maisy Herald looked up, she was maybe a little greyer and a little more war wary, but her eyes were still blue and lively and her left hand was casually on her open desk drawer. Her mouth cracked into a smile and her teeth had not changed as she had prominent upper teeth, but virtually invisible lower teeth.

"Allan! Have you come back to seek another round of lecturing on computer safety? The current lecturer is from GCHQ and he is dryer than a desiccated dormouse." She grinned. "He certainly doesn't hack into the student's phones and wake them up to Charles

Penrose and The Laughing Policeman at full volume at 3 am, which they have trouble turning off; I am surprised we weren't sued for causing unnecessary trauma!"

She chuckled, and I enjoyed the sound of her Northumbrian accent, but I could see question marks forming in her mind.

"Actually Dr Toll, I have come for some advice," I said with a smile.

She motioned to the armchairs in the corner of the room, and we sank into them.

"Fire away," she said enticingly

I tried to get my thoughts in order.

"I have been given a data mining task by a member of MI5 and a body from Military Intelligence. They say they are mole-hunting and even bought me a load of new computing gear so I could do a wide-ranging search for them. However, since it started, I've had people trying to listen in to my conversations at my home, a pair of hoods trying to warm me off with a flare-gun as I was driving my pickup, or maybe worse, and the search is turning up dozens of possibilities. It all smells wrong."

She crossed her legs.

"And your conclusion?"

I hesitated, but I was here and needed help.

"The two who are mole-chasing do not have a clue who

they are looking for but have been spreading it around I am on a red-hot trail and are using me as bait to get them to come out of the woodwork."

Her still black eyebrows rose.

"That would be just a little bit wicked."

I nodded.

"But I think they are desperate."

She rubbed her chin.

"Anything else happened to disturb your anonymity?"

I knew she'd ask, and I knew I'd have to come clean.

"I have a new girlfriend, she's Romani with a fragmented past. We think we have a complete timeline, but new fragments keep popping up that seem on the face of it to be marginally possible, so they could be using her history to unsettle me."

She sighed and shook her head.

"Oh Allan, Allan, just how did we get here?"

She walked back to the table and came back with a notepad and fountain pen.

"Who are this pair?"

"Captain Poldark from Military Intelligence and Ms Esmerelda Unthank from MI5."

Have you done a search on them?"

I opened my mouth, but she interrupted.

"I guess not, and neither should you, but I can ask a few discrete questions here and there."

Her eyes met mine and I saw the inner steel.

"Anything else?"

I mentally licked my lips.

"I was wondering about a student project."

She raised an eyebrow.

"Get them to stake out my house as if I was a deep mole. It would give them practice and show just how mind-numbingly boring a stake-out can be."

She smiled and shook her head.

"Too much risk of a mistake and I'd hate you to get shot or have your arm broken if you disturb one."

She sat back.

"On the other hand, providing invisible protection to an officer at risk is a skill we seldom train for these days, but it does imbibe certain qualities."

She leant forward.

"Have you a challenge word in mind?"

"Ezekiel," I replied. "And the reply, Nebuchadnezzar."

She smiled.

"The watchman of the house of Israel, how apt."

Her face hardened.

"To add a bit of spice, we'll cover your partner as well, but tell her the watchword and the reply and that she can shoot anyone who does not give the reply."

She suddenly switched tact.

"We'll do it for a fortnight; can you trust your cut-out?"

"I believe so, and she has been independently

recommended."

She nodded sagely.

"Very well, I will deal through them. Do not come here again and I shall have it put in the records that I invited you here to offer you a full-time teaching position, but you refused because I would not give you married accommodation."

She stood up.

"But it would be good to have you back, good instructors are hard to find; everyone seems to live for the bang, whizz, pow, but the background work is just as important." She flashed a smile. "But you now owe me one."

Will-o'-the-Wisps

Yaz stopped eating the fish and chips we had brought in.

"You have what?" She exclaimed.

I decided that I may have been a little too matter-of-fact in what I had said. I regrouped.

"I am not prepared to put you in danger, so I have called in a favour, and we should now be being watched by a group of would-be spooks. They have almost finished their training and it will be a good exercise for them and a good safety net for us. If you spot someone doing something unusual, just say Ezekiel, if they do not reply, Nebuchadnezzar then they are up to no good."

She dipped a chip in a pool of ketchup and popped it in her mouth.

"What sort of favour?"

I groaned.

"While I was recovering from my accident, I lectured at a training college teaching computer security and warning them that normally mobile phones are never safe, and computer tablets surprisingly vulnerable if you don't stay vigilant. I guess I will now have to do some guest lectures." I hesitated. "If things go pear-shaped here, we could probably move there and I could become a full-time lecturer, but it is not high on my list of possible opportunities."

She nodded and she isolated a piece of chunky batter

and gave it the ketchup treatment.

"Seen the movies; remote mansion with a front lawn full of burly men learning killing skills and inside smooth-tongued people living in the shadows."

I laughed.

"Not like that at all, though it is off the beaten track, and it is not ours, it is MI5; we are not big enough to need such a school."

She nodded and kept eating, but it was a moot distinction; I could probably be a visiting lecturer, but I'd never stand a chance of passing their medical.

Come midnight she was back in my bed, snuggling into me and raising my hormone levels.

"Suppose you did lecture there, would there be room for me?" She asked.

"Yes, but you may find it difficult to get a job unless you fancy farming or greenhouse work. Certainly, there would be no retail outlets to manage."

And, I thought, with a fragmented past like hers, they would not let her in in a month of Sundays as a potential spy who could see every person going through an MI5 training course would doubtless give the security types the screaming heebie-jeebies. She suddenly kissed me and rolled away.

"You make me feel safe," she murmured just before she fell asleep.

Yaz checked the sound system levels and we settled down for the morning service. Sitting in the back row was the woman who had patted me down in the farmhouse courtyard and a young man of similar age. They looked like any young couple and blended in well, except he found the hymn singing difficult and I thought she was going to go to sleep during the eucharistic prayer. However, they both went forward for communion, which was a mistake as they ended up kneeling in the chancel facing away from me. I casually looked around, and a tall middle-aged woman was sitting closer to me who I did not recognise and who had not gone forward. She also had a generous handbag and sensible shoes. I mentally chided myself that I should be concentrating on God, not student hunting and smiled. At one time the roles had been reversed and I had been sitting in a Baptist congregation watching a possible passer of information we did not wish to be passed, but I had listened to the sermon for five weeks in a row, until all of a sudden, I realised that there was a God, He did care about me, and I had to make a response.

While Yaz was off collecting the coffee, Rev Vera wandered in and handed me her microphone.
"Sorry, I dropped it and caught it by the microphone

cable, but I may have damaged it," she said with a smile.

"No problem, it will be easy to repair," I replied.

She gazed across the congregation.

"A little bird told me Yaz is now living at yours," she murmured.

I smiled back.

"Which little bird?" I asked.

She blinked; this was not the response she expected.

"Does it matter?"

I chuckled.

"Oh yes because I'd like to know who is gossiping about me and casting illusions."

"You mean aspersions," she replied.

"Were they?" I countered. "Casting aspersions?"

She looked me in the eye.

"Sometimes Allan you can be obtuse to the point of ridiculousness. You and I both know what I mean. I was just going to say, 'Be sure before you rush in,' but you don't rush in anywhere, do you?"

She glanced up.

"Now I must go and talk to that lady standing by the bookstall."

I put my hand on her arm.

"Message understood," I said softly.

She nodded and left. Yaz appeared and placed the coffee down.

"Rhona just asked me if it was true that you cooked a

mean breakfast," she huffed before she grinned. "I told her you liked your eggs over-easy and laid on French toast with a paprika dusting, and Brian's Café was the only place you said did them properly."

I laughed.

"Word is getting around," I remarked.

"Do you mind?" She asked coyly.

I shook my head.

"Good, because neither do I," she stated.

I watched over her shoulder as Vera pointed to indicate to the tall woman just where we had the 'singles' lunch, which, true to church tradition, did not only cater for singles and was probably a roast meal, not a light lunch.

I spent a bit of the afternoon showing Yaz how to work a Mac computer as opposed to a PC and downloading her college apps so that she could continue her college work. I also broke the habit of a lifetime and downloaded Microsoft Teams so that she could chat with her tutor group. Once she was comfortable, I left her to go back into my basement and open my safe. I put in the tin containing the dodgy smartphone and checked that I still had £5000 in £20 notes. I don't know why I check since only I use the safe, but it is a sort of habit. I then extracted a small jewellery box, inside was a ring Tekia had bequeathed me. In a note, she had said that it was her mother's and she had planned to give it to Irah on her sixteenth birthday, but now there was no one to wear it and she hoped I would find someone to wear it for me, as I was the nearest thing to a son she had ever had. It was a large flamboyant ring with a chunky square diamond in a raised thick gold setting and at least half a dozen small diamonds set into the ring on either side of the main setting. I picked up a small cloth and started to polish it while my mind was elsewhere.

Troth

I waited until 4 pm when I took in some tea and biscuits on a tray. I checked she was not talking to someone online.

"Time for a break," I announced.

Yaz obediently got up and came over to sit down on the settee next to me.

"I never realised just how slow the internet was in my old place, I only have to think it here, and it's on the screen."

I chuckled.

"Just one of the benefits of living here."

She sighed.

"When I moved in, I seriously thought it was just a temporary staging post, but…"

I decided it was time. I slipped off the settee onto one knee and held out my hand, in the centre of which was the ring.

"Would you consider putting us on a more serious footing and be my fiancée," I murmured, looking into her eyes.

She stared at the ring.

"You mean marry you?" She croaked.

"Yes, when you feel that…"

She picked the ring up and I swallowed.

"If you don't like it, I can…"

She placed a finger on my lips and then patted the settee.

I stayed where I was because getting down had been easy, but my knees only have 90° movement, so getting off the floor is not as easy. In the end, I crawled up onto the settee's arm and rolled over; she was still holding the ring.

"This is not an English ring," she said hoarsely.

I swallowed.

"I think it was made in Pakistan."

"You bought it?" She murmured.

"I inherited it."

She frowned.

"I have never offered it to anyone else and as I said if you…" I blabbed.

I stopped because she slipped the ring on her finger, easing it over the knuckle, and held out her hand to survey it.

"It definitely makes a statement," she mused.

I waited.

"You know I would want an equally ornate wedding ring," she giggled before she kissed me.

"Do you like it," I managed to say when we surfaced.

She nodded.

"This is the sort of ring my family would expect; a ring not to be ignored, a ring that speaks of wealth, a ring that shouts that I am betrothed."

"And a ring that says you are loved," I added.

She nodded and sighed.

"That too."

She held her hand out again.

"Just for the record, that is a real diamond?"

"As real as I am. I had the ring valued when I inherited it, then it was worth around eight grand.

Horror crossed her face.

"I can't possibly wear this to work!"

I held her close.

"It is a ring to be worn, otherwise how will people hear the statements it makes?"

We kissed, but the computer bleeped, and she drew back.

"My group tutor with my last assignment result," she said as she scampered across the room.

"Hello Yaz," said a posh female voice. "Are you having a good day?"

Yaz held up her hand so that the ring could be seen.

"I am having a wonderful day."

The tutor laughed.

"Well, I am about to make it better because you got an A*, which means you've passed the necessary marks and you are through to the next stage."

Yaz yelped and I smiled because I was having a wonderful day as well.

We went back to Bladon Grange for a celebration meal and, oddly enough, sat at the same table. However, the French waiter was nowhere to be seen. On the other hand, we had the same waitress, and she gave us the menus and then smiled.

"Excuse me asking, but is that ring new?"

Taz grinned and nodded.

"Today," she croaked.

The waitress's face split into a grand smile.

"In that case, you get a free glass of champagne on the house and hand-made chocolates with your coffee."

She virtually skipped away and Yaz sighed.

"She is the first person I have told."

"Second," I said. "You told your tutor."

She giggled.

"So I did."

She looked at the ring and rolled her bottom lip under her teeth before leaning forward slightly.

"The couple that have just come in, they were in church on Sunday, should I challenge them?"

I grinned.

"Let them be. We need them to watch our backs, and they probably need a square meal."

She raised an eyebrow.

"Square meal? Why a square meal?"

I shrugged.

"Some say it is because sailors used to eat off square plates and others say it comes from our American cousins meaning good, honest and proper."

She nodded and smiled.

"Since we are celebrating, I'll have the chef's steak, onion rings, chips and mushrooms."

I grinned.

"Tonight, the chef's steak is wild boar."

Horror crossed her face.

"We sometimes used to spit roast wild boar, have you any idea just how many parasites live in a wild boar?"

She shuddered.

"In that case, I'll have the slow-cooked beef stew, at least that should be well cooked."

I smiled and hoped that she was right, as last month the restaurant down the road had been fined for serving braised donkey.

Afterwards, we had coffee, and chocolates, in the small lounge. We were not joined by the young couple, but outside in one of the corridor seats there was a middle-aged man not quite dozing in an armchair; a middle-aged man I knew to be the weapons tutor at the school, somehow it was quite reassuring.

That night our resistance gave up and we made love, happy glorious love that left us worn out, panting for more, and satisfied beyond belief.

Full Stop

I decided that it was one of 'those' mornings. My search into Yaz's background suddenly halted for no reason I could discern. My police search flashed up a warning that it was beginning to search databases for the second time and my maintenance dodgers search indicated it had run through its entire list of names, while the deep search had now yielded 213 results, so it was patently useless. I restarted Yaz's search routine, plugged a new list into the maintenance dodgers search and entered details of two suspects the police wanted to find. I then attacked the search criteria for the deep search and found out that all 213 results were chosen by the same criteria from the same database, so I removed both items from the search and continued it. That all took five hours and by then both Hesp and I needed a walk.

"The drawn-out sobs of autumn's violins wound my heart with a monotonous languor," I said.
"Here are fruits, flowers, leaves and branches, and here is my heart which beats only for you," Yvette replied with a little sarcasm in her voice.
Enyo yawned and lay down, Hesp decided that this was a good strategy and lay down beside her.
"Message from your schoolmistress, 'both people are suffering from stagnating careers and met each other on a joint audit of a common facility. They are not tasked

with mole hunting and have a puny budget. Beware those seeking notoriety,'" Yvette murmured.

"Oh great," I groaned.

She casually glanced around.

"And I think you are being followed."

I smiled; she was obviously well-trained and alert.

"Short woman with brunette hair in pigtails photographing flowers."

Yvette grunted.

"On the other hand, the Major says that if someone is trying to warn you off, they might have inadvertently rattled someone's cage, so keep vigilant."

I nodded.

"And you ought to know I am now engaged," I said smugly.

She closed her eyes and took a deep breath.

"I do hope that this is the Machiavellian strategy of keeping your enemies close."

I did not reply. She offered me a packet of crisps.

"The Major wants you to have a different car," she said firmly.

"Then the Major can buy my car off me at 10% above market price as it was at his insistence I bought my own car in the first place," I said firmly.

She smiled.

"He means a second car, one with our plates and a tracker. We believe you have a charging point in your garage, so it is a Honda E with all the gizmos. It would also be better for Yaz to use to go to work, it would make her less vulnerable than she is cycling."

I laughed.

"If only she had a licence."

Yvette chuckled.

"She has; she took two tests when with the nuns for a second time. She failed the first test but passed the second, but it is only for automatics. You mean she hasn't told you?"

"I have not asked," I said.

She gave me her smug smile again.

"It is registered to her as the prime driver, the Major thought that was safer, the keys are in your crisp packet along with a memory card the Major gave me without telling me what was on it."

She stood up.

"It's parked in the Coop car park; they have a limit of three hours and I put it there an hour ago."

She wandered off and Hesp Yawned.

Following protocol, I stayed put for five minutes and was about to leave when my lass from the car park sat down beside me and made a fuss of Hesp after letting him smell her.

"Ezekiel," she murmured.

"Nebuchadnezzar," I dutifully replied.

"The drawn-out sobs of autumn's violins wound my heart with a monotonous languor," she added.

"Here are fruits, flowers, leaves and branches, and here is my heart which beats only for you," I responded.

She sat back.

"We thought that you ought to be aware that a member of your church congregation used a dead letter box yesterday."

I sat up.

"Who?"

"Woman called Rhona; she was helping at the singles lunch and one of ours was there as well. Rhona walked down Cutter Street and pushed a Specsavers envelope into a redundant shop. She could just be getting rid of junk mail, but we checked. It contained a note that just said, 'ripe for picking.' As yet, no one has collected it, but we have it under observation."

She made a humming noise.

"Want us to check her out?"

"I already have," I said hoarsely. "She is an estate agent, has an almost perfect timeline and no blots on her page but knock yourselves out as I must have missed something."

She stood up and smiled.

"You say go left, down the hill and then sharp right."

I smiled and nodded because her words had been accompanied by hand gestures. She wandered off to go down the hill, but no one followed her.

The car had a dashboard worthy of the Starship Enterprise with a screen in front of the steering wheel for essential data like speed and battery level, two twelve-inch screens side by side in the centre for a double infotainment system and two six-inch screens at the extremities of the dashboard that acted as wing mirrors, plus a smaller screen hung as a rear-view mirror. I checked the glove book and was glad to see that it only contained the service booklet and instruction manual. Going home, it felt fun to drive, but if it was a company car it would have some Kevlar inside the front doors and the tailgate, plus a bullet retarding windscreen. Otherwise, it was a sweet-looking thing that I knew Yaz would just love.

She stared at it after putting her bicycle in the garage. I got her to sit in the driver's seat and take in the ambience.

"And your lot just gave it to us?"

I decided to come clean.

"It's a company car and transport that is not registered to me but is perfect for your commute."

She chuckled.

"Park this behind the shop, Benny would go mad as it would make his van look more of a relic than it is."

"You have got a licence?" I said casually.

She laughed.

"If you are doing your job, you know I have a licence, but I haven't driven in anger since I left the convent."

"Wednesday," I said politely. "I know somewhere where we can brush up your skills."

She sighed.

"After dinner, do you think you can talk me through all these buttons and levers behind the steering wheel?"

"Regeneration," I said. "And it does one-foot driving using the regeneration as retardation."

"After dinner," she said firmly.

She suddenly smiled.

"Joe's coffee bar opposite the shop has a new waitress, the first thing she did was clean the window and the second was clean the mirror behind the counter, which I think she adjusted differently. Am I in Spooksville territory?"

"Possibly," I said warily.

As we had our evening drink, we watched the news on ITV.

"Do you know Rhona well?" I asked as casually as I could.

She rocked her head from side to side.

"Fairly well. She helped me settle into the church and we've been to the cinema a few times, nothing more.

Oh and tea together sometimes on a Wednesday when she has the day off on her rolling rota." She sighed. "Reason for asking?" she inquired.

I shrugged and she lay against me.

"You know I wish I could believe that; not regretting parting, are you?"

I shuddered.

"Grief no, I left the false glitter behind and have found my pearl of great price."

She gently punched me.

"Daft twit," she chuckled. "But my daft twit"

Unanticipated Action

At Lunchtime the following day my phone burped with an encrypted text. 'Dead letter retrieved by Lucas Archer, who has a criminal record for selling cannabis. He is not believed to be under any other influence.'

I groaned.

"Rhona, oh Rhona what are you doing?" I said to no one in particular.

Hesp looked up and I decided I'd had enough of staring at monitors, and we took a walk.

Yvette had been right, walking a dog was good cover and I walked Hesp southwards along the prom, and then west to look at a new housing development. Eastburgh Point was supposed to be hemmed in due to greenbelt policies, however, a developer had been allowed to build eighty-five houses and two low blocks of flats on what had been poor agricultural land, poor because it drained badly and was always soggy. It was an open site, and there were a variety of timber-framed houses under construction, but not a single builder to be seen. However, the show house was open and Rhona was inside with her mousy hair still tied up in a tight bun and lips redder than a pillar box. She looked up and smiled.

"You fancy a move?"

I laughed.

"Not here, no shops, GP surgery on the other side of town, the primary school already full and the houses look quite densely packed together like rats in a cage."

I swung an arm around.

"And there is no work going on."

She rolled her eyes.

"They have trouble in Stowmarket and have pulled all their staff down there. She looked out of the window.

"This will be an asset to the town."

"Do you sell used cars as well?" I said in jest.

"Misery guts," she said before frowning. "Is this Hesp? You told me you'd never have a dog."

"You told me you'd given up smoking cannabis, but I'm guessing you are growing it in that Edwardian wreck of yours."

She gave a crooked smile.

"It is a house with potential, I've started to get builder's quotes and the first two would be manageable, but I'm hoping the third will be a bit cheaper."

"But it still has a serviceable basement," I persisted.

Her eye narrowed.

"Are you trying to give me a message?"

I decided to bite the bullet.

"Whatever you are doing stop now, the police are not idiots, and you may feel you have all the bases covered, but can you trust your supply chain?"

"It's medicinal," she said huffily. "I grow it for MS

sufferers."

I turned away.

"Tell it to the judges, but I doubt they will listen."

I turned back for one last try.

"This is not fifteen points on your license and a nine-month ban meaning you have to walk everywhere: this is a criminal record, how would your boss view that, what would it do to…"

She held up a hand.

"I have already pulled out; I can't have builders in and tell them to ignore the basement when all the utilities come in there."

I nodded and made for the door.

"But thanks," she called after me. "You do have a heart after all."

Hesp plucked a bloom from the ornamental rose bush outside the door, and then peed on the stem, I knew just how he felt.

We walked home and I left Hesp to take the little Honda to pick up Yaz as I wanted her to get used to it before she started driving it. I drove to her shop and circled to go down the dingy side street behind the shops to park beside Benny's old faded red Renault van. I could not get in via the back doors, so I made my way down the somewhat grubby street to see Rhona coming the other way, doubtless walking back to her estate agents. It was at this point that mayhem ensued. First, a small motorbike with two black-clad riders with black full-face helmets and tinted visors turned into the street and roared along to park in front of Rhona while the passenger leapt off and started wielding a nasty-looking knife. I could not hear what he was saying, but it did not look polite. Instinct took over and I ran over the road and pushed the static motorcyclist over, I caught him unawares, but even so, he managed to swipe my face on the way down. I think I shouted at the second guy who was threatening Rhona, but my voice was drowned out by a black Transit van turning into the alleyway to stop and disgorge at least four armed policemen. The driver of the motorbike tried to get back on his machine and make an exit, but a police car drew alongside me blocking him off. A rather burly policeman in all the necessary kit for an armed response pointed his gun at me.

"On the floor and on the floor now!"

I carefully took my hand out of my pocket and showed my ID card.

"I'd rather not," I said conversationally. I have two artificial knees so to go on the floor means I'd have to fall down, and once down I probably can't get up without help."

Over his shoulder I could see a young man had appeared and was filming the proceedings, the driver of the van leapt out to remonstrate with him as he held up his ID card by his camera and said something to him. My PC frowned and growled.

"MI7, pull the other one; down and down now."

Out of the corner of my eye, I could see that the two black-clad youths were on the ground and relieved of two rather large knives and a knuckleduster. Rhona was being held against the wall by a stocky WPC and the PC who had challenged the cameraman was rushing over to the sergeant in charge.

"Call it in," I said firmly. "Or the egg is on your face."

He reached for his radio.

'Control, an ID check please," he intoned.

"Not over a plain radio," I hissed.

He looked startled and stepped back as the sergeant ambled over.

"Stand down," he muttered as the photographer eased himself behind the police van and disappeared.

The sergeant came over to me, grabbed my arm and took me to one side; he smelt of vindaloo and chocolate. "I'm told we are disturbing an intelligence operation," he said in a low voice.

"Not interested in the two low life," I said softly. "But go easy on the girl, she feeds me information without knowing it."

He raised a grey eyebrow.

"She's an estate agent, even terrorists need somewhere to rent and usually they are not normal clients."

He nodded as if what I had just made up made sense. He glanced around.

"We know she is involved in a cannabis factory and probably has some on her," he murmured as one of the other policemen opened the top box on the bike to extract a bag of used fivers and another bag of cannabis wraps.

"Will it stick in court?" I replied.

He gave a half smile and turned around.

"Those two in the van," he ordered as he ambled over to Rhona and shushed the PC away.

He had a 'friendly' talk to her and then, as swiftly as they had arrived, the bike was pulled into the van, and they all drove off.

Rhona was white-faced and trembling and looked at me with hysterical eyes.

"How did you do that? You had some sort of ID card that made them back off," she said tremulously.

"What did the motorbike guy say?" I asked.

She swallowed.

"That it was a Hotel California, and I could check in, but I could not check out, or else."

'And the police sergeant.?" I murmured.

She shuddered.

"He said I was on their radar, gave me a verbal caution and told me that next time I might not be so lucky, but this time I was fortunate to have a 'friend' in high places.'"

Her eyes widened.

"What do you do? You never told me what you do!" She half shrilled.

I smiled.

"I save friends in distress, but I can do it only once."

I went to walk away and hesitated.

"I'll walk you to your office."

We set off and I chose my words carefully.

"I work for the government on specialist IT investigations. We look for oddballs and people with grudges. If you rent one of your flats to an oddball, you might like to tell me."

It wasn't far and we reached the back entrance to the estate agents that were on the other boulevard. She left my side and paused to unlock the door, but she was shaking so much that she had trouble putting the key in the lock. Eventually, she opened the door and looked at me.

"Thanks," she grunted. "But Yaz is welcome to you."

I got around the front as Yaz was closing the front door.

"Just in time," she said.

She peered at my face, which was beginning to throb.

"What happened to you?" She asked as her eyes widened.

"It's a long story," I said. "But let's go home first."

Skid Pan

I watched as the Honda E pirouetted on the skid pan and decided that I never wanted to be a driving instructor. So far Yaz had had half an hour pottering around the old runway perimeter track and doing a couple of emergence stops. An hour of instruction in real traffic and was now 'enjoying' the skid pan. For the second time she tackled a curve, and this time completed it; I guessed that the instructor had turned all the safety gizmos back on. She went round a second and third time at a faster rate, until on the fourth nothing electronic could save her and it was down to old-fashioned driving techniques. Eventually, she drove back to the portacabin where I had been enjoying some coffee and climbed out; I could see that she was 'buzzing' with the experience. The instructor, a burly policeman with a wrinkled face and the patience of Job smiled at me.

"Your turn," he said. "She's a good little gal and can take a fair bit of misuse, but when she breaks away it could catch you out."

I hoped he was talking about the car.

Yaz drove us away from the centre.

"Enjoy that?" I asked.

"Terrifying, but I liked it," she responded.

She glanced in the mirror.

"When we were out, he tried to teach me some observational skills, do I need them?"

"I sincerely hope not," I replied, hoping that she had not noticed that we were being carefully followed by a green Fiat 500 with the 'young couple' from the church in the front seats.

She turned into our street and my observational skills came to the fore.

"Drive past," I hissed.

She glanced at me as the Fiat behind turned into the road and made a hash of parking between two cars, I hoped as a distraction activity. I pulled out my phone and dialled a number.

"Casual securities?" I asked.

I got a grunt.

"Client 295, there is a…"

"We know," came the reply. "Fly swatting due any minute."

"Would you mind just telling me where to go and why? Snapped Yaz.

"Into town and the carpark behind the library," I answered. 'And it's because there was a white Mercedes SUV with tinted windows parked three doors down from our house and they are the type of vehicle a certain sort of spook just loves. It could just be an innocent family, but it is best to be sure."

She groaned.

"I've seen the movies; you mean the CIA."

"And Mossad, plus the French, Italian and Greece agencies, but oddly not the German ones as they think the connection is too obvious."

She reached the town centre and turned into the car park. Two minutes later a nondescript green Peugeot entered and parked a little way away.

"Now we wait," I said.

We sat there for half an hour, hardly talking. Suddenly a moped turned into the carpark, parked near us and a parka-clad figure climbed off to wander over and climb in the back seat.

"Yaz, this is Yvette, a colleague," I murmured.

"The one from the firing range," she replied tartly.

Yvette's eyes flicked between us.

"Since Yaz is temporarily on our books, I can talk to both of you. We ascertained that at least five people were sitting in the Merc and called out the armed police. You will never guess what they found."

"Border Agency," I said.

"More spooks," said Yaz.

"Five bonafide MI6 Agents," she said with a smile.

"They have no jurisdiction over…" I started.

"Who are all now detained by the police on firearms charges, plus carrying the usual paraphernalia for breaking and entering, including a police scanner, but we contacted the police by phone and asked them to keep radio silence."

"They must be desperate," I said.

Yvette smiled.

"They will be since the police have already complained to the Home Secretary," Yvette said with a smile.

Her smile disappeared.

"I have been instructed to accompany Yaz home and stay until your return. You are ordered to interview the MI6 team leader with a police Inspector present and ensure that it is a recorded interview." She licked her lips and passed me the crash helmet. "Speed might be of the essence."

I knew what she meant, if the PM got involved, we could all be ordered to return home and count everything as a non-event."

The interview room was a grim beige room with just a table that could seat six and the obligatory recording machine. The police had provided Detective Chief Inspector Greta Thomas, which suited me as I could understand her North Wales accent. We sat down and a chap calling himself John Janus was led in to sit opposite us, while the burly sergeant stood against the wall behind him. Grata started the tape machine and read through the preliminaries while I laid my smartphone on the desk with a red dot clearly showing. She looked at John, a fifty-something scrawny man in a tweed sports jacket and blue jeans with a thin sunken cheek face containing a flattened nose. She smiled at John.

"Shall we cut the crap? Your fingerprints identify you as Matthew Moulder, an MI6 operative."

"It is illegal for you to tap into our database," he snarled in a Newcastle accent and leaving a faint smell of tobacco smoke in the air.

Greta smiled.

"We did not need to interrogate any database but our own. You were caught driving while talking on a mobile phone and refused a roadside breath test. You then refused a blood sample citing MI6 immunity while on duty. You were charged with both offences and your prints were taken. You have not had your day in court; hence your fingerprints stand."

He swore under his breath.

"You are refusing a solicitor?" She inquired.

"Don't bloody need one," he sneered. "I'll just wait for the phone call to end this charade."

He leant forward.

"Otherwise, it is a 'no comment.'"

She leant back.

"I would advise a solicitor," I said softly. "Because treason is a serious charge."

He just sneered at me. I tried to nod sagely.

"You are being thrown to the wolves. Someone ordered

you here and it would not be them spending time in HM Prison Wakefield, it would be you."

He scowled.

"Have you got a paper trail of your orders? Were they certified? Have you any proof you were not acting off-piste on your own initiative?" I said softly. "On the other hand, I am searching for an MI6 mole in the knowledge that they may well try and stop me from doing so." He blinked. "Acting as bait and waiting for the fly to call," I added quietly.

His grey eyes flitted between us, but neither of us said anything.

Suddenly Greta laid a Luger pistol on the desk.

"Not standard issue," she said matter-of-factly. "Serial number filed away, other identifying marks equally removed. The perfect weapon for a hit. I believe they are called shoot and toss."

"It's not mine," he croaked.

"Really?" Greta said with an air of disbelief.

He closed his eyes and I prayed that there would be no phone calls to save him. He took a deep breath.

"I was ordered to break in and wreck the basement and if possible torch the place, but he has a bloody great guard dog, and I was not authorised to go around shooting dogs. We were waiting for him to return home and take the dog for a walk."

"Ordered by whom?" snapped Greta.

He took a deep breath.

"My boss' boss, Fredricka Salisbury-Smyth. She told me it was a special off-the-books mission."

"Interview paused," said Greta, giving the time and date.

Outside Greta smiled at me.

"You got enough because he is one red hot cookie?"

I nodded.

"Was the pistol his?" I asked with a smile.

She smiled back.

"We found it tucked away behind the glove box."

I grinned as I remembered the mantra from training college, 'Always search your vehicle because you never know who had it before you.'

"I need a private room, pronto, before I have to delete that recording," I said urgently.

She took me through a security door and pointed me down the hall.

"Use my office."

I smiled and walked towards the office, but I had a problem because Fredricka Salisbury-Smyth was the major's wife.

Difficult Decisions.

I sat for three long minutes weighing the pros and cons of who to call, but it was a no-brainer. I dialled a number. It was answered swiftly.

"Allan here. Weather forecast for Jupiter's South Equatorial Belt: cloudy with a chance of ammonia," I said hastily.

"I don't love the world, I think Jupiter should have hit us," came the reply.

"Encrypt, JJ1," I said hurriedly.

There was a beep on the line.

"In place," she said.

"The police picked up an MI6 team outside my house, thanks to your students. I have just interviewed the team leader, and he fingered Fredricka Salisbury-Smyth as giving him orders to trash my work area and torch my house. It is only his word, and we are expecting a wipe-out call at any moment," I blabbed. "But I can hardly call it in."

"Can you play me the interview?" She asked.

I played her the recording.

"Your thoughts?" She mused.

"Too easy," I replied.

She laughed.

"Oh far too easy. I know Matthew and he is as cunning as a fox, as wily as a wolf and not prone to breaking down under a gentle interrogation. He has thrown you a googly, but I will note this call, just in case you get run over by a friendly bus," she chuckled.

"Is he trustworthy?" I asked.

"As any of us," she replied enigmatically. "But yes, I would trust him if I had to. Glad my team is of use, keep smiling."

She rang off and I sighed with relief.

The weary PC opened the cell door for me and walked away, clearly he did not like people in my type of organisation. Matthew was lying on the shelf they call a bed and as he saw me he swung upright.

"Had a little call, have we?" He said with a chirp in his voice.

I walked over and sat down next to him.

"Not yet, but we both know it will come and we both know you've been spinning fairy tales and that you wouldn't care about any dog."

He smiled but did not reply.

"We are supposed to be on the same side, so you just tell someone you can trust that a pair called Captain Poldark and Esmerelda Unthank are shaking the tree to see what falls out. We all know there are moles and subversives, otherwise, we would be out of a job, but now the tree is shivering someone is rattled. It could be a mole, it could be an ambitious toad, or it could just be someone with malevolent intent making us face the wrong way. They are playing games and frankly, we haven't the time to waste."

He grunted.

"You were one of us, I came across you in Berne at some international conference and you were working with the Danes; I have to say you looked very cosy."

I kept quiet.

"Tried to look at your file," he mused. "But it's been ringfenced, now why would that be? Friends in high places? Perhaps you have information that might be helpful to outsiders? Maybe it's political?"

I didn't reply.

"Give me something," he hissed.

"There is a new diplomat in the Brussels Swedish Embassy called Persson; look up my data file on her, you may find it interesting. It is encrypted using the standard hexadecimal rolling code," I replied.

I heard footsteps approaching.

"Anything for me?"

"I'll test your goods first," he grunted.

"And tell me, is Padlock Securities one of yours?"

He hesitated.

"Military Intelligence," he murmured as Greta peered round the door.

"The Home Secretary has given us a call; it's all been an interdepartmental training exercise and is not worthy of recording."

Her eyes flicked between us.

"One day we might trust one another," she sighed. "But not today."

I found Yaz and Yvette sitting with their feet up in the conservatory sipping tea with the two dogs lying contentedly on the sunny lawn. Hesp looked up at my arrival, thumped his tail on the grass and then closed his eyes.

Yvette stood up and clicked her fingers. Enyo jumped into life and trotted towards her.

"I guess it was a good interdepartmental training exercise," she said sweetly.

"Of course," I replied.

She smiled at Yaz.

"Thanks for the tea. I'll see myself out."

I sank into a chair.

"I am sorry, you didn't expect this," I sighed.

She rolled her eyes.

"Oh, it's a wild ride. I've learnt how to kill people through a brick wall using a shotgun, whizz about on slippery surfaces and be suspicious of every stranger who parks their car within a half-mile radius."

I opened my mouth, but she reached between chairs and held my hand.

"On the other hand, we have found one another, and

that is worth a small fortune."

I knew what was coming.

"But any children we have could not live like this," I half-groaned.

I squeezed her hand.

"If it passes, all well and good, if it doesn't, I'll seek something else."

She squeezed my hand back and then held on for a moment.

"You go and do your spooking in your den, and I'll cook dinner, then let's give Hesp a good walk.

Downstairs the deep search had now turned up 136 results while nothing else was producing anything of note. That allowed me to sit and think, rather than just react. In the end, I decided that my pair of opportunists were not the only ones who could go around shaking trees.

Windfalls

It took two days to set it up, calling in a few favours on the way, but in the end, I had a meeting at the training school early Friday afternoon. Matthew and I were sitting in a small interview room that had four armchairs and two hidden CCTV cameras. They walked in and looked around before sitting down. This time Esmerelda was wearing a beige cloak, but I knew she should not be hiding anything as she had been frisked by the tutors on her way in and passed through a metal detector. He looked the same and glared at Matthew.

"I was under the impression that we would be alone," he said testily.

"I would not have come if I had known the indignity we would be subjected to," she snapped.

I laughed.

"If you were truly MI5, you would know what to expect because you would have been here, or somewhere similar for your training, except you transferred into MI5 from the Office for Security and Counter-Terrorism following a debacle over what is best termed legal misinformation."

She scowled.

"My companion is Matthew Moulder from MI6, and I asked him to accompany me for reasons that will become apparent," I added.

Captain Poldark looked around.

"Is this being taped?"

"Yes," I said truthfully. "As I have some rather interesting results from your search," I added, somewhat untruthfully.

Esmerelda sat bolt upright.

"You have?"

I nodded.

"135 hits of which 85 are for the same person."

"Really?" said Poldark. "On the data we gave you?"

I nodded.

"Eighty-five hits for one Esmerelda Unthank, so I can only assume you set me running to see just how secure you were."

Her mouth dropped open.

"But Belarus," snarled Matthew. "Just what possessed you to work for them? Or is it just a back door into Russia? Is that where your true affinity lays?"

She turned white.

"But I..."

"We have the evidence," I said. "But we are not quite sure of the involvement of Captain Poldark in all this. Data would indicate that he is complicit in..."

"Don't be stupid man!" he snapped.

"Not stupid, but highly suspicious, still it will all come out in court, although the proceedings will be in camera due to the sensitive nature of the evidence," I said while trying to keep a serious voice.

I patted Matthew on the shoulder.

"Mr Moulder is here because it was his agents that were 'removed from office' following your leakage of information."

Captain Poldark tossed his head.

"You have nothing on me other tha…"

"Padlock Securities," I said lightly.

His eyebrows rose.

"You cannot possibly think that I…"

He closed his eyes.

"You have an alternative explanation?" I murmured.

They stayed quiet.

I nodded sagely.

"In that case, we have the Military Police and the Anti-Terrorism Unit outside and…"

Captain Poldark's eyes flitted between us.

"I fear we are rumbled m'dear," he sighed.

"An admission of guilt?" asked Matthew, a little over-sarcastically.

"Not guilt," she snapped. "Rattling the tree because of a financial anomaly we found."

"Financial anomaly!" Matthew roared. "You tied up my whole team because of a financial anomaly!"

"You'd better come clean," I murmured.

Captain Poldark licked his lips.

"We were asked to do an audit of the MI7 part of the JIO, nothing too rigorous as we are aware of the grey edges surrounding slush funds, bungs and some operational activities, however, we found a safe house, or rather two safe houses when MI7 is not listed as having any."

"One turned out to be your house, the ownership was not declared, but the utility running costs made us suspicious, had they listed it as a data centre we would not have blinked an eyelid, but a safe house was another matter," said Esmerelda haughtily.

"And the other?" Matthew asked, somewhat roughly.

"Ah," said Captain Poldark. "That is where it gets interesting."

He glanced at me.

"They run a facility they call Blenheim House, which is obviously training suicide bombers, judging by the spending and cross-agency acquisition of explosives and the indoctrination training of some of its operatives. The problem being that if we disclosed it, it would probably disappear in the blink of an eyelid."

I groaned.

"It is a training school to teach people how to deal with suicide bombers and what to look for as standard MI5/6 training only treats it superficially, leaving the disarming of such bombs to the army. However, if you get to the point of trying to talk down a suicide bomber or disarm him while you have him or her pinned down, you have failed as far as intelligence is concerned."

Esmerelda blinked.

"You know about it!" Said, Esmerelda.

I smiled.

"You know I know about it as I used to be stationed there."

Captain Poldark nodded.

"And you also had links with the PLO."

I groaned again.

"Mossad, I worked with Mossad, but it was pointless because if they see someone whom they think is a suicide bomber they are more likely to shoot first for self-preservation reasons than try to capture alive, but their intelligence gathering was worth studying."

Matthew suddenly woke up.

"It was set up following a terrorism select committee realised that suicide bombers, especially the loners, needed further and more careful study in response to a couple of off-grid characters causing mayhem at public events."

Esmerelda turned white.

"We thought you were the recruiting arm, so we decided to raise your profile in the hope that…"

"Other agencies took an interest, and you were exposed," added Captain Poldark.

"And Padlock securities?" I asked harshly.

"Just jollying things on a little, to make you more exposed."

I sat digesting this before Matthew spoke up.

"Where did you get the money?" He growled.

They looked at each other.

"We're auditors, we know where the bodies are buried," Esmerelda said simply.

Matthew, Maisy, and I sat in her office drinking coffee, which had not improved in my absence.

"You're saying that this pair of idiots ran an internal black ops operation in the belief that a perfectly legitimate facility was off the books and working against MI5 and MI6!" Maisy said in amazement.

"That is what they would have us believe," said Matthew. "But they have had plenty of time to compose a cover story."

"And they needed help, I doubt that either of them would know how to generate a false border crossing, complete with passports and photographs," I added.

"They have the money and the contacts," muttered Maisy. "They did not have to do it themselves."

I shook my head.

"They knew I was checking out my partner, only a few people knew that, and they were not on the list."

"You had written confirmation to do this?" Asked

Maisy.

"Verbal, straight from my Major's mouth."

"So, the list is?" She asked, head on one side.

I thought about my answer.

"The Major and my handler, plus anyone the Major told, which is unlikely."

"Short list," said Matthew.

I shook my head.

"I cannot believe they have even met either the Major or my handler."

Maisy closed her eyes and sighed.

"I have an answer, but you are not going to like it."

"So do I," Matthew replied.

She smiled.

"You first."

"Your partner is a plant from another organisation, and the Major knows it.," he said flatly.

"Unlikely," I said. "Her backstory is too complicated, and he would have had to get a nun to lie to me."

Maisy laughed.

"Which just leaves my theory; you're being pressure vetted for a top job and your partner is a potential fly in the ointment."

I blinked.

"What job?"

She smiled.

"Let's go and find out."

Pressure Vetting.

Captain Poldark eyed Maisy with suspicion.

"Maisy Herald, director of this institution," I said, by way of introduction.

She smiled at them both.

"You're blown; neither of you is really what you say you are, and I've taken the liberty of having this morning's mugs taken to the fingerprint lab, just to verify my thoughts, but you are not Military Intelligence and MI5, you are from the high echelon vetting team."

Esmerelda's lips compressed into a straight line.

"That is like calling us…"

"Cut the crap, you're blown," snapped Maisy, making us all jump.

"You couldn't possibly expect us to…" Major Poldark started, but Esmerelda touched his arm.

"We would like to have finished the job without discovery, but yes, we run a vetting unit within GCHQ and were asked to re-establish the vetting status of Mr Parks in the light of certain developments within the security establishment and because of his dalliance with one Miss Klempár."

"I will not go back on active duty," I said flatly.

Captain Poldark smiled; except we now knew that he most definitely was not Captain Poldark.

"As I understand it no one is expecting you to, in any case, we do security vetting, not medical fitness examinations, as we all know where we stand there."

"For?" I asked.

He shook his head.

"Above my pay grade and…"

He petered off as a young woman came in, handed Maisy a note and walked out. She smiled.

"John Smith and Jane Doe from GCHQ building maintenance, I would have expected nothing less, but you are indeed GCHQ."

Esmerelda stood up.

"Our work is done and…"

"Please sit down, another couple of questions to humour us," Maisy purred.

She hesitated and sat down.

"Just to ease our minds, it was you trying to bug Allan using his conservatory window as a microphone?"

"Check," said Esmerelda, somewhat gruffly.

"And we would have maintained a watch if he hadn't called out the cavalry."

"And you set the border agency onto Yaz," I snarled.

He raised his hands.

"Not guilty, but fortuitous." He hesitated. "But we were forewarned that it was going to happen, however, I am of the opinion that the ladies' eviction from their trailer was not engineered by anyone, again it was fortuitous."

"Pull the other one," Matthew replied.

They both just smiled and stood up.

"We shall go now, I am afraid that none of you shall see our report," Captain Poldark murmured as they left.

I let out a sigh of relief as they closed the door, Maisy chuckled.

"I wouldn't relax if I was you."

I raised an eyebrow.

"High-level pressure vetting costs money and uses up resources, so someone, somewhere, has designs on you."

Matthew laughed, and I groaned.

I didn't even make it out of the college grounds as I found the Major sitting in my pickup. He tapped his smartphone.

"Got your vetting report last night as our couple from GCHQ knew they were rumbled the minute you invited them here."

"I'm happy doing what I'm doing," I said.

"And you're damned good, doing what you are doing," he replied. "And if it isn't broke, why should we all waste money trying to fix it?"

I waited.

"We are just extending your remit to check up on judges and politicians, not necessarily our own."

"Isn't that illegal?" I remarked. "They are elected."

He shook his head.

"Following that debacle last year when three English

MPs and four European MPs were running a cabal involved in illegal immigration and the attempted export of uranium by a couple of misguided magistrates, the Supreme Court has ruled that such vetting is in the interests of the state. However, they also ruled that such checks should carried out in one place, and not by MI5, MI6, GCHQ, or Military Intelligence." He patted me on the shoulder. "Which means the JIO MI7 and you." He sniffed. "But you can maintain your cover of seeking out divorce miscreants."

He looked me in the eyes.

"Yvette has also been vetted to a higher standard and she will remain your cut-out, but Pete is out of the frame because he has a daughter dancing for the Bolshoi."

He grabbed a door handle.

"Now go back to your domestic bliss, we will talk again about extra security and a bit more computing power as there is an election coming up."

He climbed out and shut the door, I noted that he hadn't asked me if I was prepared to do it.

Reset

When I got home, I picked up Yaz and took her out for a meal, after all, I had a lot to tell her, and a lot not to tell her.

Also by this Author:

ABOUT THE AUTHOR

IvanB is a retired Telecommunications Engineer and a retired Anglican Minister. He lives in the wonderful county of Suffolk and enjoys life by the sea. Writing is a hobby, but an absorbing one.

Printed in Great Britain
by Amazon